"Lady, they're  at nothing t

"Do they want   to keep her voic   was shaking with h

"They'll take you aead, but I think they want you alive," Austin said. "At least, so they can publicly execute you in the capital square."

Tarini swallowed hard.

"Don't worry," Austin said in that damnable we're-doing-it-my-way voice. "I'm going to keep you away from them...for the baby's sake."

"Austin, maybe I better explain—"

"Don't bother," he said dismissively. "I don't have time for explanations. You might be important to others because of some ancient monarchy garbage, but you're important to me only because you're carrying my best friend's child. No other reason, understand?"

Dear Reader,

As a novelist, I am surprised every morning when I turn on the computer. Characters that I thought certain to do one thing decide most emphatically that they will do the opposite. Situations that were pretty straightforward the afternoon before take a decidedly Gothic turn. And sometimes characters who have a small but nonetheless pivotal role in one book announce they have their own story to tell.

It was while I was writing the November 1996 Harlequin American Romance novel #655, *Marrying Nicky,* that Tarini Schaskylavitch demanded her own book. When single father Nicholas Sankovitch entered into a "green card" marriage with Toria Tryon to resist deportation to his native land, it was countrywoman Tarini—special agent to the U.S.—who afforded Nick the opportunity to live up to his wedding vows.

For all that hard work, Tarini wanted her own chance at romance. And two very special editors, Debra Matteucci and Denise O'Sullivan, agreed. But Tarini is no ordinary heroine—she's a woman of mystery and danger. She needed a whole new category for her story. Luckily, there's Harlequin Intrigue.

My best,

Vivian Leiber

His Kind of Trouble
Vivian Leiber

Harlequin Books

TORONTO • NEW YORK • LONDON
AMSTERDAM • PARIS • SYDNEY • HAMBURG
STOCKHOLM • ATHENS • TOKYO • MILAN
MADRID • WARSAW • BUDAPEST • AUCKLAND

ISBN 0-373-22416-8

HIS KIND OF TROUBLE

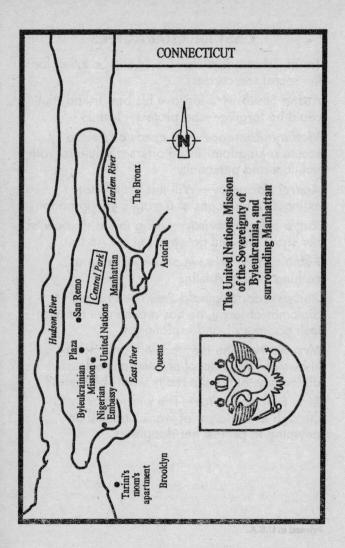

CONNECTICUT

Hudson River

The Bronx

Harlem River

N

San Remo

Central Park

Plaza

Manhattan

Bylekrainian Mission

United Nations

Nigerian Embassy

East River

Astoria

Queens

Brooklyn

Tarini's mom's apartment

The United Nations Mission of the Sovereignty of Byleukrainia, and surrounding Manhattan

CAST OF CHARACTERS

Tarini Schaskylavitch—Could she be killed for the secret she carries?

Austin Smith—He forgave his best friend, but could he forgive—and protect—Tarini?

Vladimir Romanov—He needs an heir to secure a kingdom. Tarini offers a solution, both political and personal.

Andrei Karinolov—Will this brutal man extinguish the hopes of a fragile young nation?

Tanya Schaskylavitch—Living in the shadow of her sister, she will do anything for Andrei.

Bob Kearner—He swears he will stop at nothing to help Austin.

Ambassador Reginald Smith—A retired diplomat-at-large, he has a penchant for high-tech gadgetry...and espionage?

Mrs. Smith—The devoted wife and mother knows all the protocol of international diplomacy. But is she really what she seems?

Mrs. Schaskylavitch—The widow has lived through every terror of war...and will do anything to protect her daughters.

Prologue

January 7, 1997
Byleukrainia

As the aerial assault on the city began, some of the soldiers in the trenches felt fear. Others a rush of adrenaline. Still others, an unleashing of their dark, primitive selves. But Andrei Karinolov felt none of these emotions. His only emotion was a possessiveness for a city that would soon be his. He simply stood behind the safety of the bunkers, and watched the bombs fall on the helpless city. He spared not a moment's thought or pity for the innocent lives being destroyed.

"Necessary," he would have said if asked.

Once the city fell, Andrei would travel across the Atlantic to bring back the last traitorous Romanov. And then he would stand to gain a country and a city and a people.

But, most of all, he would bring the woman to

her knees before him. He had promised himself the woman. Because she was very much like him— strong-willed and proud—Karinolov would enjoy breaking her as he would a fine Thoroughbred. He marveled at how soon she would be enslaved by him.

He remembered the touch of her skin. Soft as silk, the color of café au lait. Her hair he remembered as blue-black, and her eyes like emeralds.

She would be his reward.

And from her, he would bring forth his own dynasty.

January 7, 1997
New York City

SHE FELT the cold, clammy touch at her cheek and she screamed.

"Tarini, Tarini, wake up, you're having a nightmare."

Jerking her head around, she opened her eyes to the sapphire blue eyes of her lover, Austin Smith.

He held her from behind, his hard, damp legs entwined with hers, the scent of their lovemaking lingering in the tangled Egyptian linen sheets, the traffic sounds of Manhattan drifting up to the penthouse apartment overlooking Central Park.

"You were having a nightmare," he consoled.

Tarini Schaskylavitch shuddered with embarrassment—she didn't like this unwilling display of her weakness.

She was sure that Austin didn't, either. Austin liked their relationship clean, uncomplicated—the carnal sparring of two sexually sophisticated equals.

Equals with no past.

And no future.

She thought of the nightmare—just a smattering of images from her youth. An odd touch to her cheek that provoked such revulsion. So much haunted her from her early childhood in Byleukrainia. Her widowed mother had sacrificed greatly to get her two daughters to the safety of the United States. Tarini remembered everything, too well, in fact. Her sister, Tanya, had been a toddler and had no memory of those difficult years before they came to America.

Austin turned on the light. The bedroom was white, with plush pillows and soft, thick comforters. Comfortable and yet masculine—an antique map of Cape Horn and a series of framed black-and-white photographs decorated the walls. A sleek glass-and-steel desk flanked the bed. The windows were covered with rice paper screens and a screen door opened to the dressing room and bath.

As the son of retired U.S. diplomat-at-large Reginald Smith, Austin had lived all over the world and his sanctuary showed his appreciation for the many cultures and customs he'd encountered.

"Come here," he said, drawing her to him. He caressed her legs, quickly chasing away the memory of her dream, bringing pleasure in its place. She was as physical as he was, though she was not nearly as sophisticated.

He entered her just as she was ready for him and they came together in pulsing, driving passion that chased away the darkness and exhausted them both. They fell into a calm, dreamless sleep.

Tarini awoke in the morning to an empty bed. She pulled on Austin's work shirt, discarded in the previous night's lovemaking, and walked up the spiral staircase to the rooftop conservatory of the penthouse apartment. Austin was working out on the treated-pine flooring and glass panels he had built himself. Potted early crocuses and paper white narcissus dotted the courtyard. He kicked, blocked and punched in the combinations prescribed by traditional Shoto-kan karate.

Tarini sat at the wrought-iron table where Austin had laid out a tray of her favorite black tea, and a platter of buttery croissants still warm from the oven.

He had always been thoughtful the morning after intense lovemaking.

She fixed herself a plate and watched Austin work out.

Austin was a man of the world, with cultured tastes in wine, cuisine, automobiles and women.

She lived at home with her mother and sister—and was in awe of everything Austin had to show her.

About life.

About love.

All right, admit it, she thought, she was in awe of everything Austin had to show her about sex. And, from what her married girlfriends had hinted about sex, he was an unusually gifted lover.

She had come into this relationship with her eyes open. Austin wasn't a settle-down kind of man. And she had no intention of marrying outside of her Byleukrainian community—her mother would hit the ceiling if she did.

Their relationship had, at her request, been kept a secret. Her traditionalist community would scorn her had they known. And Tarini was determined to protect her mother and her younger sister's reputation. They had been careful about where they went, how long they stayed wherever they went, how they acted when their paths crossed in public.

There was no talk of love and no talk of a future.

She hadn't wanted either of those things when they first met. She had been surprised by her wanton surrender to him and even more surprised by how quickly she had come back for more.

Now everything had changed, although the rooftop conservatory with its potted boxwood and bonsai spruce looked as eternally lush and serene as the day before, although Austin's glistening chest and

arms worked the same karate moves as they had the
day before. The Manhattan streets were still covered with a thin dusting of the New Year's snow.

Only Tarini was different.

She swallowed hard just thinking about the future. She had thought she was past the trouble spots
of her life. But now, in just the past day, her world
had been turned upside down.

But she was a survivor.

She'd figure out a way.

She pulled his shirt closer around her shoulders,
feeling a scratchiness in the pocket of the otherwise
soft cotton fabric. She felt a piece of crumpled paper in the shirt pocket, pulled it out, looked at it
and felt her cheeks burn.

She looked down at the phone number scrawled
in loopy, feminine script. He hadn't made any
promises and she had no right to confront him.

If she talked to him, told him everything, she was
sure Austin would do the right thing—but for how
long and with how much resentment?

She took a sip of the burning hot tea.

As if there had been any doubt about telling him.
She knew only one man to go to. Vlad would help
her. The young United Nations ambassador from
her homeland was like an uncle to her—her grandfather had fought in his grandfather's army, her
grandmother had spirited Vladimir's own mother to
safety when the Communists took over and her fa-

ther had died fighting to protect Vlad's father. The family ties were cemented by a personal affection.

But Austin and Vlad were friends, the very closest childhood friends. Would going to Vlad destroy the bond between the two men?

She put the piece of paper into the pocket of Austin's shirt and went downstairs to get dressed.

She left the apartment before Austin finished his workout.

January 9
Byleukrainian United Nations Mission, New York City

THE UNITED NATIONS MISSION *for the Sovereignty of Byleukrainia is pleased to announce the engagement of the Honorable Ambassador Vladimir Romanov to private citizen Tarini Schaskylavitch. They will wed February fourteenth in a traditional ceremony to be held at the mission.*

Ms. Schaskylavitch is a native of the mother country and has worked as immigration liaison to the ambassador for the past two months. She was posted with the United States Immigration and Naturalization Service in Chicago and is notable for saving the life of Byleukrainian environmental scientist Nicholas Sankovitch and his American bride Victoria Tryon.

Ambassador Romanov is the last direct descen-

*dant of the Byleukrainian Romanov dynasty and
is...*

Austin crumpled the memo in his fist and cursed
Tarini's name. An innocent? Hardly. She had
played him for a fool. Claiming they must keep
their relationship a secret because of a traditionalist
family—and he had honored her desires.

Forget it! Forget her!

January 14
The Ambassador's Suite, New York City

SHE MUST HAVE BEEN two-timing him all along, luring Vlad into a marriage alliance while coming to
Austin for more...carnal pleasures.

Barely days after she had left his apartment, after
she'd declined to take his calls at her office—he
now knew why—she had risen from his bed to
place the Romanov diamond engagement ring on
her finger. And he had actually worried that he had
done something to hurt her feelings!

She had acted like a viper, a— But here he
stopped himself. He hadn't made any promises, and
had never asked for any. He wasn't that kind of
man. And while he wanted to warn his friend Vlad
what sort of woman Tarini was, he figured Vlad
already knew well enough about his bride-to-be.

After all, this was not a love match. Tarini was
descended from a long line of high-ranking Byleu-

krainian aristocracy. A marriage would be regarded as a triumphant reemergence of the Royalist movement—although the military now threatened to take over the tiny breakaway republic on the Black Sea.

The dark-haired beauty Tarini and the impeccably pedigreed Vlad would be a perfect political couple. As an American, he confessed that he could barely comprehend the importance of these unions. As the son of an American diplomat who had been posted all over the world, he knew these alliances could change the course of a country's history.

No, he shouldn't warn his friend. He should simply offer his congratulations. He ran his fingers through his hair and touched the tiny amplifier in his ear. He heard the crackle and hiss and then a sudden clarity.

He reminded himself he had a job to do.

In his mind's eye, he reviewed the layout of the mission—every stairwell, door and window. And every weakness. He thought of the men he had under his command and where he had placed them. Then he buttoned the suit jacket of his tuxedo and gave a last tug at his black silk tie.

Working out the wording of his reluctant congratulations, he took the secret stairwell to the private penthouse apartments of the mission. He found Vlad standing by his valet tray, his eyes glued to the television, scenes of the battle for the Byleukrainian capital casting an unholy light against the walls.

"How can you watch that stuff?" Austin said, flipping off the television and closing the heavy teak armoire that contained it. He reached down and picked up from the Aubusson rug the diamond-encrusted cuff links Ambassador Vladimir Romanov, with his shaking hands, had dropped.

"It's my country. I fear for it."

Austin slipped the links through the stiff linen cuffs of Vlad's sleeves. He studied the lines of worry and the paleness of his friend's face—Vladimir felt so intently every tragedy of his people.

Did he understand that he had his own life to consider, as well?

"Sorry," Vlad said. "Never could get the hang of these things."

Actually, both Vlad and Austin had worn black-tie so frequently in their thirty years they could dress blindfolded.

"As security adviser for the mission, I'm formally requesting that you cancel the ball," Austin said. "I can't guarantee the safety and security of the mission and its personnel."

"You're still mad about the metal detectors."

"Vlad, I'm mad about you not letting me do my job," Austin said, reining in his emotions because he was unsure how much of it was the desire to shake his friend by the shoulders and tell him not to marry the scheming, wickedly beautiful Tarini. "Vlad, every other day of the year, you follow my security procedures. It means the difference between safety and death."

They both paused, thinking of the assassination attempt two months before. Austin had ended up with an arm in a cast—but Vladimir had been hustled to safety with no more than a scrape.

Austin had done his job well.

"Tonight is different," Vlad said. "We can't put guests through the same security checks that airline travelers endure. These are representatives of sovereign nations, diplomats, even a few royalty."

"I'm not talking about security for them anymore," Austin said. "I'm talking about your safety. Your capital is burning. Your democratically elected government is going down in flames. You need to consider...your personal options. I have a contact at the State Department standing by and a safe house in Connecticut, and—"

"There is no 'personal' in this, Austin," Vlad interrupted. "I am nothing more and nothing less than a servant of my people. That's what being a Romanov means. Generations ago it came with a crown."

Austin sighed regretfully. How he wished he could protect Vlad from the realities of the world.

Like the other Romanovs, Vlad didn't have a good sense of self-preservation, a selfish survival instinct that Austin knew was an inherent part of himself. In fact, Austin had often wondered if he could ever be as selfless a servant to his people as his friend was.

Probably not.

There were only three people he'd consider laying down his life for: his mother, his father and Vladimir Romanov.

That left a little less than four billion people on earth out of luck.

Parting the heavy golden damask curtains, he looked out onto the mission's cobblestone courtyard. A parade of black limousines with tiny flags flapping at each corner paused at the ornate wrought-iron gate to the official residence of the U.N. ambassador. Drivers leaped from their seats to open their passengers' doors.

The crowd was thinner than expected—as Vlad stood at his shoulder, Austin knew his friend was looking for the American ambassador's car, and he calculated that the ambassador's absence was an ominous sign.

Still, nearly three hundred guests crowded into the courtyard, waiting to be announced at the door. They were drawn by loyalty to the courtly Ambassador Vladimir Romanov, coupled with simple, nearly morbid, curiosity about the regime that was toppling halfway around the world.

Austin turned away, letting the heavy curtain fall

into place. He tugged at the too-tight collar of his starched white shirt.

Though he wore black-tie often, he didn't feel comfortable in anything but his favorite pair of blue jeans and one of the team jerseys from his college days.

"You're determined to do this?" he asked.

But he already knew the answer, and in a very important way, if Vlad were more of a realist, their friendship could never have survived. Austin admired his friend's adherence to his own code of honor—without it, Vlad was nothing. Austin grudgingly admitted that he'd have to live with his friend's recklessness this evening.

"I also have my engagement to announce," Vlad said, unaware that his friend had stiffened. "When I give the traditional toast to Tarini, I would like you at our side."

Not on your life, Austin thought. *I wouldn't stand next to that…witch if my life depended on it.*

But it wasn't his life. It was Vlad's life and his country. And their friendship, which spanned nearly two decades and was closer than any two brothers'.

No two-timing, scheming, lying woman was going to destroy their friendship, Austin vowed.

"PERIMETER ONE, check," Austin said softly toward the mike at his shoulder as he followed Vlad down the staircase from the private apartments of the mission.

"Perimeter one, check," came the reassurance at his ear.

"Perimeter two, check," Austin ordered.

"Perimeter two, check," replied one of his hand-picked guards.

Vlad and Austin passed through the second-floor gallery of treasures.

"By the way, I received a telecommuniqué from the Belgian ambassador," Vlad said. "He threatened an international incident if he has to send his daughter home to Brussels because of her infatuation with you."

"Perimeter three, check."

Austin glanced distractedly at Vlad, waiting for the reply at his ear that didn't come.

Belgian ambassador's daughter?

Then he remembered. She'd given him her phone number. He'd put it in his shirt pocket.

Then he had lost the phone number. Just a few days ago. Hadn't given it another thought.

"Relieve the ambassador's mind by telling him I only go for blondes," Austin said, reminding himself that he had always had a preference for blondes.

Tarini had been the exception. No more exceptions.

"Perimeter three, check," he repeated, tapping the tiny microphone.

Vladimir took his position at the top of the winding marble staircase that opened to the ballroom. As he stood, the string quartet brought the Bach to a close and the guests looked up.

"Austin?" Vlad said in a voice so like a child's.

"I'm here, buddy."

Vlad reared back his shoulders and raised his hand in a formal salute to his guests.

"Perimeter three, check," Austin said more urgently, touching Vlad's sleeve as a warning not to walk down those stairs until he was sure of the safety check.

But as his fingers touched the rich fabric of Vlad's tuxedo, Austin caught sight of her.

Tarini. Zipped into a white sequined sheath that puddled around her ankles, she was regally tall, with boyishly slim hips, voluptuous breasts and skin the color of palest café au lait. Her blue-black hair had been sleekly rolled into a chignon at her neck. Her eyes were the color of the rare tigereye emeralds that adorned the simple necklace she wore on her exposed neck.

She had the striking allure of the sexiest lingerie-catalog model coupled with the sophistication of a Manhattan socialite.

And she had a five-carat diamond on her left hand that made her strictly off-limits.

Still, after all she had done to him, her eyes sought his. What was there? Was it scorn? Was it pride? Or did he detect regret? He met her gaze head-on.

The moment caught him off balance. Vladimir slipped from reach. The guests burst into spontaneous applause as he took the hand of the British ambassador in greeting. The noise, reverberating off the cavernous ballroom ceiling, made it impossible to hear.

"Perimeter three, check," Austin repeated, pressing his transmitter tightly to his ear. "Charlie, are you there?"

Nothing.

Vladimir held out his arms to Tarini.

Austin felt an exploding sense of foreboding.

He ran down the stairs two at a time, tugging at his friend's shoulder just as Vlad's lips touched Tarini's mouth.

And then, with a roar of gunfire, all hell broke loose.

AT THE FIRST SPRAY of gunfire, Tarini's heart leaped to her throat and she reached for the gun that wasn't there. Too late, she remembered how she had thought an ankle holster would ruin the line of her luxuriously body-skimming evening gown. And, besides, as immigration liaison, it wasn't her job to provide security. That was Austin's job.

She looked up to the staircase and saw three masked gunmen flying down the steps, raking bullets over the heads of the stampeding guests. The crowd bolted through every available exit, one woman leaving a single pale pump teetering on the floor, another losing her purse in the melee. Someone toppled over a crystal balloon vase of lush flowers. White, astringent-smelling spray flew in an arc as a waiter dropped two champagne bottles. Broken glass, water and smashed hors d'oeuvres littered the ballroom floor.

She looked around frantically for Vlad. He must be saved!

"Get down, woman!"

Someone shoved her to the ground so hard the air was knocked from her lungs. Sequins and delicate beads popped from her gown and scattered across the marble floor like confetti. The weight on top of her rammed her hips into the marble floor. She coughed, trying desperately to regain her breath. She tugged and cursed and shoved and then her eyes met those of the lead weight on top of her.

Austin. He looked at her, eyes registering disgust, and then rolled off. He slipped a cartridge into his gun.

"Don't shoot anyone, Austin!" Vlad's quavering voice pleaded.

As Austin released her, Tarini tugged her skimpy strap into place. She looked up in horror at the staircase. Vlad stood surrounded by four assailants. A single rivulet of blood ran down his cheek.

"Don't shoot," he repeated. "Austin, put down your gun. Otherwise, there will be carnage. It's me they want."

Austin glanced at Tarini with devastating hatred. Tarini knew exactly what he was thinking—if he hadn't squandered precious moments throwing her out of the line of fire, he could have done his job protecting the ambassador.

"Please, Austin, put it down," Vlad said, his voice regaining some of the dignity that had made him one of the most persuasive speakers in the United Nations council chambers. "These men are serious. They want me. Please, just ensure the safety of my fiancée."

Again, Austin looked disgustedly at Tarini.

The room lapsed into tense silence. From beyond the closed mahogany door came the murmur of panicked guests. From outside the high, leaded-glass windows the sounds of sirens from a distance.

The police. But they wouldn't enter the mission without the direct invitation of the ambassador.

Diplomatic posts—whether consulates, embassies or missions—are considered the exclusive and sacred lands of the country to which they belong. The New York City police would no more enter the United Nations Mission for Byleukrainia than they would invade France.

"You're going to have to give up your weapon, Austin," Vlad said quietly. "They're going to shoot me if you don't."

"I can take them."

"Not without an innocent life at risk."

Austin spared a dark look at Tarini.

He obviously didn't regard her as particularly innocent.

"Austin, as the ambassador of this mission, I order you to relinquish your weapon."

With a wounded grunt of frustration, Austin slid his gun across the floor to the men at the staircase. He stood and sullenly held his hand out to help Tarini to her feet.

Gripping his fingers, she teetered uncertainly, the heel of one of her pumps having broken off in the chaos.

"You can't get away with this," she told the terrorists with lilting bravado. "I have worked as a special agent with the American government and I can assure you that the United States takes a hard line on—"

"Oh, Tarini, shut up!" Austin snarled. "You're not helping matters any."

Tarini glared at him.

He ignored her.

"What is it you guys want?" he demanded.

"Just put your hands up," one of the men said gruffly. "And wait for further instructions."

Tarini obeyed quickly, but Austin hesitated. One of the men lifted his automatic to order compliance. Austin reached to a pocket on the right of his jacket. A staccato crackle as Austin fired. A masked terrorist fell three stairs to the floor. Austin had taken him out with a clean shot to the arm.

Tarini tried to move, willing her legs to go, go, go—but, she was frozen with fear and shock.

Lightning quick, another assailant leaped from the stairs and yanked her to the ground beneath him, hand clamped over her mouth. She couldn't breathe, and she panicked, clutching at the man's visor grip.

Out of the corner of her eye, she saw Austin grab Vlad, yanking him up from the floor and leveling his small handgun at the remaining gunman.

Inwardly, Tarini cheered.

Austin fired several shots but didn't hit his target. He hustled Vlad toward the door. With the last ounce of her strength, Tarini willed herself to squelch the desire for breath and instead concentrate on gripping her captor. She had to keep him down.

Austin had to make it to the door!

He had to get Vlad to safety!

If she could hold on just one second longer, they would get out...

"I've got her!" The man on top of Tarini screamed. "I've got the girl!"

"Fine!" Austin cried out, shoving Vlad ahead of him toward the door. "Keep her!"

But as Austin shoved the ambassador closer to the exit, Vlad pulled out from under his friend's authoritative hand.

"We can't," he said.

The room was in an eerie standoff. Austin and Vlad poised at the door. Tarini held to the ground. Three gunmen—one wounded—uncertain what to do.

"You want Tarini, you can have her!" the gunman holding Tarini cried out. "But you gotta give us the ambassador."

"No way!" Austin growled.

"Don't give him up, Austin!" Tarini cried.

With great dignity Vlad walked to the staircase. Austin made to follow him, but the gunman on top of Tarini held his weapon to her forehead, the barrel pressed against her skin.

"I'll shoot her if I have to!" the man screamed so close to Tarini's ear that her head throbbed with a sudden and terrific pain.

She closed her eyes and tried to remember the words to the prayer to the saints that her mother had taught her.

"Pity you have to die, babe," the malicious voice said.

"All right, all right," Austin exclaimed. "Take the gun off her."

Austin threw his remaining handgun to the ground, but his blistering oath in Tarini's direction made clear that he wasn't at all happy.

The weapon still grazing her hair, the gunman pulled his hands away from her mouth and nose. Tarini shivered and wiggled out from under him.

At the foot of the stairs, the assailant who had taken Austin's bullet moaned. The sirens seemed closer...

And upstairs came a high-pitched squeal and then the *tap-tap-tap* of the ambassador's fax machine.

"Word from the capital!" Vlad cried out.

"Won't do you much good," an assailant said, snickering.

And then the machine fell silent.

Someone was in the diplomatic apartments—their footsteps skittered overhead.

Tarini gasped at the sight of the man who appeared at the top of the stairs.

Andrei Karinolov, a hero who had fought the Communists and gained a large following in Byleukrainia, sauntered down the steps with the unconcerned, breezy air of a late-arriving but well-honored guest. He was followed by three men who struggled to carry a large wooden-slated crate. On the crate was the Byleukrainian seal and the official stamps identifying the crate as the possession of the diplomatic courier.

"What is the meaning of this?" Vlad demanded, retaining his supreme dignity.

"You have been called back to your country, Ambassador Romanov," Karinolov answered. He directed his men to open the crate. "Get inside."

"You can't do this!" Austin shouted. He rose and punched the man to his left with a hard jab— the man crumpled to the ground with a grunt.

On Karinolov's direction, the three armed men leaped to overpower Austin, and shoved him onto the marble. One grabbed Austin's hair, battering his face against the hard floor until Austin's nose bled and an angry welt covered his forehead. He took the punishment without complaint, but when his eyes met Tarini's, she could see the mixture of pain and humiliation that he couldn't take them all on.

Then his tormentors yanked up Austin by his shoulders for Karinolov's appraisal. One eyelid was cut. His right arm hung at a funny angle.

Tarini ached inside, fighting the urge to cry out for mercy for him.

"Austin Smith, you are a very worthy opponent," Karinolov said with mirthless laughter. "And I would dearly love to set you free on the mission's grounds and track you like a dog. We could have such fun. Of course, you'd die."

"So do it. Set me loose, right here. I'll take you on," Austin challenged, sucking back the blood dripping from his mouth. "But do it like a man.

One-on-one. You choose the weapons or lack of them. But without your goons."

"I'd love to. But when we finished, you'd still be a dead American. How touchy the State Department gets when a single, worthless citizen is harmed. So, tonight, you'll just enjoy a little cocktail I've prepared for you so that I won't have to deal with your primitive loyalty problem. We'll meet again in other, more private circumstances where I can...play. But not tonight."

He pulled a hypodermic needle from his breast pocket, flicked a single air bubble from it and walked over to Austin.

"Let him go," Austin urged, spurting blood all over Karinolov's shirt. "If you want, I'll fight you for him. You and me. Winner takes Vlad."

"And the weapons?" Karinolov asked blandly, looking with distaste at the red splatter marks on his turtleneck.

"Anything you choose."

"A charming offer, but I'm afraid I'll have to decline," Karinolov said. "Our country is being swept up in history and this Romanov is too important for me to game for him. Tonight was the only night we could get to him—your security arrangements are ordinarily so...thorough."

"I'll take him away, I'll make sure you never hear from him again," Austin pleaded. "He'll spend the rest of his life without a political thought in his head.''

"Sorry, Austin, you'll have to go on your own. Have a nice trip," Karinolov said, shaking his head.

He jabbed the needle into Austin's forearm.

"You'll never get away with this!" Austin warned. "The State Department will bring you down. There'll be retaliations. Killing an ambassador—"

"I'm not killing him. I'm simply recalling him."

"In a crate?"

Karinolov shrugged. "A lot of Royalist traitors to Byleukrainia have made him a cult figure. They might plan rallies at the airport, attempts to free him. We can't have that. A crate eliminates so many unpleasant possibilities. We know he'll reach his destination."

"He's protected by the Vienna Convention as an ambassador." Austin slurred his words, but valiantly grasped at straws. "You'll be arrested. The police are on their way."

Karinolov laughed. "The police? The police can't even give me a parking ticket."

"Why not?" Tarini asked.

"Because they can't touch me," Karinolov replied easily. "I have the one thing that makes all this legal."

"And what's that?"

"Diplomatic immunity."

"I am the only person in this room with diplomatic immunity," Vlad said.

Karinolov dropped a sheaf of papers at Vlad's feet. "The military has taken over the capital, and the war hero—that's me—has been chosen to plead our country's various causes at the United Nations. I have a following, you know." He paused before adding, "Not only do I have diplomatic immunity, but any package that bears my diplomatic seal cannot be opened by another country's officials. It would be an act of war and America has no intention of going to war with the world's biggest supplier of uranium."

Tarini closed her eyes to the horror of it, knowing full well that the diplomatic immunity of a United Nations ambassador covered everything from parking tickets to murder.

And also knowing that Karinolov and the others of the military takeover did have a following, a large following who believed his hard-line rhetoric.

Her own sister Tanya, for instance, kept a photograph of Karinolov in her bedroom and mooned over him as if he were a movie star.

But, then, in public and on camera, Karinolov always seemed so charming and heroic.

"Allow me to introduce myself more formally," Karinolov continued. "I am the new ambassador to the United Nations for the Sovereignty of Byleukrainia."

Austin shuddered and slipped out of the arms of his captor. His body went limp. His facial muscles relaxed. He slumped to the floor and Karinolov gave him a sadistic kick on the head. Austin kept his eyes on Vlad, but his body had failed him.

She let out a breath she hadn't known she had been holding. She had wanted Austin to be the knight in shining armor. To save Vlad, if not herself. Now she knew. There was no hope.

There was only herself.

Tarini stood up to face Karinolov. "You're the new ambassador?"

"Yes. As of this moment."

"Where are you taking Vlad?" she demanded.

"Why? Do you want to go with him?"

She only needed a moment to consider the offer. "Yes, I would," she said, knowing that her duty was to protect Vlad. With her life, if necessary.

"No," Vlad said quietly. "Tarini, I must go and you know why you cannot follow."

Their eyes locked. His so sad and worn, as if he were much older than his thirty years.

The ambassadorship had been meant by the recently installed prime minister to be a training school for Vladimir. Someday, so the plan had gone, Vladimir would take his country's helm. Not as a king as had once been his birthright, but as a democratically elected leader. He was a popular figure and would unite the people.

All that was lost as the military regime must have taken over. Tarini wondered what fate the prime minister had met this evening. Death, most likely.

"It's all right," Vlad said gently. "I've been expecting this. I knew something horrible must happen here if the military took over. Stay, Tarini. And please tell Austin that I know he did everything he could and that I'll hold him to the promise I just extracted from him regarding your safety."

And with unwavering stateliness, Vlad climbed into the diplomatic crate as if it were a limousine. His last smile was brave and poignant as a leather face mask was snapped on and the restraints tied to his arms and legs.

"Vlad!" Tarini screamed.

The last nails were hammered into the crate. Then the diplomatic-courier seals were affixed to the lid, identifying it as protected under the Vienna Convention by order of the new ambassador.

Tarini watched, horrified.

Karinolov came to her, his breath at her ear.

"I'm so sorry that we finally meet again under these circumstances," he said, reaching out to touch her cheek. "You are still as beautiful in the flesh as—"

Revolted, she slapped him.

Instinctively, he responded by crushing his handgun against her head.

She tumbled into darkness, feeling a stab of de-

spair as she knew that she, like Austin, had failed
Vlad.

"Austin," she murmured with her last conscious
breath.

Karinolov stood over Tarini, solemn and still.

Austin. He was positive she had said, "Austin."

He looked back at the bodyguard, who had
slipped into unconsciousness. How he despised the
American.

Then Karinolov stared at her limp body, at the
black hair that spilled onto the pale marble tile. He
felt a wrenching sense of betrayal, and everything
he had felt for her exploded in a red-hot rage.

"Get her out of here," he ordered his men.

Chapter One

Austin stared at the tree buds opening on the Strawberry Fields section of Central Park, which lay beyond his apartment window. April *was* the cruelest month, reminding him of life when all he could think of....

He crushed his empty beer can and free-threw it to the wastebasket beside his desk. He missed.

Powerless. He felt powerless. He had never had experience with that emotion and he didn't like it.

He rubbed his two-day stubble. None of his contacts in Washington would recognize him now. Gone was the pressed shirt and the charcoal-gray suit, the confident and determined swagger, the tough and rugged smile that had been his trademark.

He had spent two months doing everything a man

could do—in the halls of State Department, anonymous smoke-filled cafés in Washington, the CIA complexes in Langley, West Virginia, and the top-secret National Security Administration offices in Fairfax, Virginia.

And he had come home in defeat.

Vlad had disappeared, swallowed in the chaos and confusion of the beginning days of the military-led government of Byleukrainia.

Tarini had disappeared, as well, not that he wanted to see her. Not that he cared.

"Hey, buddy, you gotta move on," Bob said.

Austin glanced at his friend, whose stocky frame was dwarfed by the plush leather Zulu throne Austin's father had brought to America from one of his more exotic government postings.

Bob must know what he felt, Austin thought. He had stood outside the mission that night with twenty-three other squad cars. The officers had calmed petrified party guests, cordoned off the area from press and gawkers, escorted everybody to their cars and surrounded the perimeter of the mission.

But there wasn't a thing Bob Kearner could have done for the people inside. Even for his buddy Austin.

Stepping into the mission was the equivalent of crossing a border into a foreign country. Violating their diplomatic entitlements. Creating an international incident. Bob had told Austin many times how he would have liked to have thrown away all the rule books that terrible night, especially as Karinolov's limousine had glided out from behind the wrought-iron gates, taking Vlad to Kennedy Airport.

"Austin, I know the last two months haven't been easy," Bob said, putting the discarded beer can in the wastebasket.

"It hasn't," Austin agreed bitterly, though he was ordinarily not a man who complained. "My best friend has been kidnapped and is either dead or—worse—in a Byleukrainian prison. And our government won't do a thing about it because the kidnapper is covered by diplomatic immunity and we'll recognize any government which will grant us access to those uranium mines."

"It's bad, I know. But if you give up on yourself, you'll never be any help to him."

"It was my fault in the first place."

"Stop torturing yourself. Nothing could have stopped them. They knew the Winter Ball was the only time they could get around your security system. They knew Vlad would take risks and so they crashed the party to get him. You know all that. Maybe they could have just as easily caught him on the street."

"You're wrong. On the street I could and would have protected him," Austin muttered, replaying out loud a tape that had been stuck inside his head from the moment he had awakened in the Manhattan alley where the kidnappers had dumped him. "I shouldn't have let him go on with the ball. I knew I couldn't protect him. He refused the most minor inconveniences of security for his guests. I failed him—and that was not just my job, it was my promise as a friend. I broke that promise, that trust."

"He was being foolish," Bob said. "Any other man would have gone into hiding when it looked like the capital was about to topple."

"Any other friend would have dragged him into hiding."

"You did everything you—"

"It was all because of a woman," Austin interrupted. "Tarini. His safety should have been our only concern. Instead, both Vlad and I were thinking of her. I grabbed for her, to pull her to the ground out of gunfire, when I should have fired. I lost those seconds—those seconds may have cost Vlad his life."

"Where is Tarini, by the way?" Bob asked, edging cautiously forward in his chair. "I mean, do you keep up with her at all?"

Austin shook his head. "No."

"Where is she now?"

Austin scowled. "If she's anywhere on earth, it's not far enough away from me."

Bob sighed and sat back in the buttery leather

cushion. "I didn't just come here to cheer you up," he said quietly. "I need a favor."

"What?"

"I'm starting my own company," he said, pushing his wire-rims higher on his nose. "A little moonlighting because you know I can't raise three kids on a cop's salary. Simple security operation. I've got a party on Saturday to cover. Give me some of your time. Six hours, tops."

"The last time I did security for a party, the host got kidnapped and the guests had a terrible time," Austin said dryly.

He raked a hand through his sandy blond hair. He needed a haircut. Bad. But he didn't have the energy to do anything about it.

"Please. It's a diplomatic party. Everyone's bringing their own bodyguards. It'll be a madhouse. You're the only one I know who can make it go."

Austin groaned. "No way, Bob. I've had enough of that crowd to last me for several lifetimes."

"C'mon, Austin. I really need someone who knows how to set up a perimeter of safety. I gotta have someone who can wire a house. And I gotta have somebody who knows the protocol. You know I only know two languages—English and Brooklynese. You're fluent in eight."

"Nine," Austin corrected. "I've been brushing up on my Swahili."

"See? You're perfect for the job."

"Forget it, Bob. Besides, if I were a diplomat, I wouldn't hire me."

"Everyone knows it wasn't your fault. They're all running scared, Austin, they've seen something terrible happen. So now even a barbecue at the Nigerian mission requires a virtual SWAT team."

"And where do you fit in?"

"A little guy like me is just in the price range of a third-world country with a U.N. mission to protect. If I do this job well, I'll get other jobs. I need the money. You don't know how bad."

Austin looked out the window. They were dusty, needed cleaning. The whole apartment needed hosing down. How'd he let it get to this? Out of the corner of his eye, he noted Bob fidgeting in the Zulu throne. Shifting his weight, tugging at his belt, grimacing as his back raked the prayer bells that hung from the chair.

Bob had asked him a favor. A friend with a favor to ask couldn't be sent away empty-handed. But he shuddered at the idea of going out of this apartment, even for a moment, to face the people he had known for so long—in his new role as a failure.

But suddenly, his mind started racing.

"Will Ambassador Karinolov be there?"

Maybe there was something to the law of vengeance.

"Maybe," Bob said, and his eyes skittered away. "But don't count on it. He's being snubbed."

"Snubbed?"

"The diplomatic community is snubbing him. He didn't even get invited to the secretary-general's Spring luncheon and the mayor refused to seat him for the Pavarotti concert."

Austin rolled his eyes. "I'm sure the new ambassador is devastated."

"Come on, Austin, just say you'll help me out," Bob pleaded. "Consider it a favor for a friend. Your goddaughters want to go to ballet school this summer and the fees are killing me."

Austin regarded his friend critically. Years before, there had been gambling debts, so steep that Bob had been nearly forced into bankruptcy. Austin had paid them off. The subject of repaying Austin had never come up, because a policeman's salary would never allow for it. It had simply been a favor between two friends. Austin would do it again in an instant if Bob asked.

But would Bob ask? Or would he be too ashamed to return to his friend a second time?

Austin hadn't thought about Bob's gambling problem for a long time. But he shook his head as he studied his friend's placid face and he knew he couldn't ask. He didn't want Bob to think he was dunning him for the repayment of the money. Besides, surely he would have seen other signs if his friend was in trouble...

"Ballet lessons?" Austin said, clapping his

friend on the shoulder. "You drive a really hard bargain."

THE NIGERIAN MISSION was housed in a small, crumbling graystone across from the Eldridge Street Synagogue on the Lower East Side. Far from the regal missions of the wealthier nations, it still managed to convey its own special charm with a colorful flag flapping in the breeze and its door emblazoned with the Nigerian crest.

Ambassador Abu Dikko, wearing a traditional Yoruban robe of pink and white, stood in the foyer, prepared to greet his guests. His attaché hovered behind him, ready to direct people to a spacious dining room where a buffet of fragrantly spiced foods was laid out. A band in the heated courtyard played the brisk, finger-snapping juju music of King Sunny Ade.

At the kitchen table, Austin spoke firmly to Bob's handpicked security team of off-duty New York City cops. Detailed blueprints of the mission, as well as maps of the surrounding streets and alleyways, were laid out in front of them. Ignoring the chatter of the kitchen staff, Austin reviewed for a final time the locations team members would take, where they would move as the party progressed and the weaknesses in the building's structure which must be defended if necessary. Every contingency was allowed for, every disaster anticipated.

Austin remembered why he liked this business—
it was like a puzzle, figuring out how to secure the
building, how to ensure the diplomatic community
solidified their personal relationships with comfort
and ease and a sense of safety. Those personal relationships were the building blocks of international
cooperation, so Austin didn't for a moment think
of any party as trivial. Balls, receptions, teas, din-
ners—they were where the real work of diplomacy
was done.

Each member of the team wore a tuxedo and
plain black satin tie. Bob tugged uncomfortably at
his collar and repeatedly cleaned his glasses with
the silk sleeve of his jacket. Austin made a mental
note to tell Bob he needed to become more comfortable in a dinner jacket if he expected to work
with this echelon of society.

Austin would blend into the crowd with an un-
derstated tuxedo and a close shave. His hair was
cropped astronaut-short and his cheeks were still
red from the five-mile run he'd taken.

As the time of the party approached, he had
pushed away all thoughts of the last diplomatic
party he had covered, focusing on ensuring the Nigerian mission's safety and his hope that Bob Kearner's first job would go well.

He'd always had a soft spot for Bob's daughters.
If they wanted ballet lessons this summer, well,

he'd do the job and take them to buy new leotards, too.

"All right, men, you know what to do," he said at last, gathering his meticulously drawn blueprints and maps and putting them in Bob's briefcase. "And if we do our work well, Bob's phone will be ringing off the hook Monday morning."

The men dispersed throughout the mission, linked together with transistors wired behind their ears.

Austin checked his gun. He used the subcompact because it was small and its safe-action system ensured no misfires. The gun fit into the palm of his hand, and yet, it carried a lot of power. Forty-caliber power. Austin had customized his weapon with a LaserClip gunsight, a panel on his barrel that activated a powerful beam of light to aid in precision aim.

Austin put the gun into his shoulder holster and prayed, as he did every time he wore it, that he wouldn't have to draw and fire.

With a nod to the giggling waitresses congregating at the kitchen door, Austin took his position near the foyer. For the next two hours, he quietly shadowed the host, Ambassador Dikko.

And if the ambassador felt queasy about placing his fate in the hands of the man who had guarded Vlad Romanov, he never let on. Dikko smiled and chatted and shook hands and never once looked in Austin's direction.

That was how good security worked.

When Austin turned over to Bob the responsibility for tailing the diplomat, Ambassador Dikko was dancing in the courtyard, his robe swaying and his feet tracing intricate patterns on the stone tiles. It was a party like any of the thousands Austin had attended at his parents' many homes or in his own work—and yet, he could feel the unfamiliar sense of fear.

Eyes darting to and fro. A worried glance exchanged over cocktails. Mouths occasionally tightened in quiet anxiety. A grim determination to have fun—laughter too loud and faltering before it stopped abruptly.

Bob was right—the community had been spooked by Vlad's kidnapping.

As Austin walked to the dining room where a bucket of ice and cola beckoned, he heard a commotion in the foyer. A group of gray-suited, pasty-faced men parted and allowed their leader to emerge.

Karinolov.

In the past two months, Austin had played out in his head a half-dozen ways of confronting the ambassador. Meetings in his mind that, he would have been ashamed to admit, ended with Karinolov dead or at least begging for his life. In every daydream,

Austin was cool and calm and without remorse or mercy.

Now Austin's mouth went dry and he wasn't nearly as composed as he would have liked. Still, he put his hands to his hips and stared boldly at the man who had kidnapped his friend.

"So we meet again," Ambassador Andrei Karinolov said with a courtly bow.

It was possible, just barely possible, to imagine the charm that made Karinolov still such a popular figure in his homeland and among some members of the American immigrant community.

Austin suppressed the blinding urge to simply fire. It would be so easy—the gun was holstered only inches from his fingers.

He could take Karinolov out in less than a second. But years of training and a personal sense of honor stopped him from shooting dead an unarmed man. Even if the man was Karinolov.

Instead, he shrugged with forced nonchalance.

"Ambassador Karinolov, I would say it's a pleasure to see you. But it's not. So I won't. This is a private party. You have not been invited. May I show you the door?"

Karinolov smirked. His entourage hesitantly mimicked their leader's humor and guffawed uneasily. Karinolov quieted them with a withering glance.

"Step aside, Austin, and thank your Lord above that I didn't shoot you when I had the chance."

Austin touched the transmitter at the back of his ear, signaling backup.

"This is a private party," he repeated. "And your name doesn't appear on the guest list. I must ask you to leave immediately."

Karinolov shook his head. "Oh, I think Ambassador Dikko will be delighted to have me," he explained airily. "There are eight thousand Nigerian nationals working in the Byleukrainian uranium mines. I think their safety and continued welcome in my country is worth a little hospitality, wouldn't you agree?"

"No, I wouldn't," Austin said. He felt Bob at his side and, beyond the French doors, he noted three team members surrounding Dikko. The guests had begun drifting toward the far courtyard wall, not panicking but clearly uneasy. The Nigerian ambassador stared expressionlessly at the unfolding drama in his foyer—he had been through many times of turmoil and wasn't easily ruffled.

Austin's fingers worried his holster. He glanced at Bob, who had gone white as a sheet.

"There are two reasons why you'd never harm me," Karinolov said archly. "One is that you are a man who believes in law and in honor."

Austin felt Bob pull at his sleeve. Irritated, he glanced at his friend—if Bob would just leave, he'd be tempted to pull the gun now and be done with it.

But Austin wouldn't put him in danger. Wouldn't leave a widow and two fatherless girls.

Because Austin had no doubt that while he'd get the first shot and it would fire true, he wouldn't get the second shot or the third shot or the last.

He didn't care if his life ended tonight, but Bob was different. He had a family to think of.

"Sometimes the law doesn't work," Austin said evenly. "That's when honor takes over. A man can believe in one but not necessarily the other."

Karinolov looked him up and down as if seeing him for the first time.

"You've changed a little in the last two months—you've lost that all-American look and that all-American belief that the good guys always win. There's something darker about you. Maybe you could pull that trigger—oh, but I forget. There's still a second reason you'd never lay a finger on me."

"What is it?"

"Vlad is still alive."

The words took a moment to sink in. And then Austin felt his heart soar. Alive! He had given up all hope.

"Don't think we're releasing him anytime soon," Karinolov cautioned. "When we finally take out the last of the Romanovs, we're going to do it in a very public, very splashy way. Now, if you'll excuse me, I have a party to attend.''

He brushed past Austin and walked across the woven jute rugs of the receiving room.

"By the way," Karinolov said over his shoulder. "How's that beautiful woman of yours? Her name was Tarini. If it was in my power, I'd trade you Vlad for her. She would give me even more pleasure than the opportunity to shoot Vlad myself.''

Austin's blue eyes narrowed with distaste. And with shock. Their relationship had been a secret.

"How did you know about—"

"Tsk, tsk, tsk," Karinolov chastised, eyeing the buffet table with apparent interest. "And Tarini was such a tease, wasn't she? Always made a man feel like he was the first. I once loved her, once long ago. But then I learned.''

Austin felt the blood pounding at his temples. He had never asked about her experience and Tarini had never volunteered any information. He had reasoned that she must be sophisticated and sure of herself. And yet, something deep inside had often wondered at the fresh, innocent quality she brought to their lovemaking. Had it been an act? Had Tarini shared Karinolov's bed, as well?

"I wouldn't mind trading her for Vlad, myself. But Tarini wasn't my woman," Austin said firmly. Even her name tasted bitter on his lips. He had awakened too many nights with her image burning in his mind—and he had applied every ounce of self-discipline to forget her.

Karinolov stopped abruptly. He spun around, his face twisted with puzzlement.

"What do you mean, she wasn't yours?"

"She was engaged to Vlad," Austin replied. "If it weren't for her, I could have gotten him out of the country that night before you arrived. I might have saved him. At the least, I would have reached for the gun instead of throwing her out of danger."

"Is she carrying his child?"

Austin startled. He hadn't even thought of that possibility. When she'd been with him, she had been very careful about birth control. Had she been trying to have Vlad's child at the same time? Was their wedding a conjunction of her pregnancy and Vlad's sense of honor?

"I...I don't know that she was pregnant," he said, the question catching him so off guard that he didn't stop to think what effect his candor would have.

"Would it have been yours or his?" Karinolov asked.

"Or yours?" Austin countered, recalling both Karinolov's slur and the way Karinolov had been so entranced by her that night at the mission. As if they had met before. As if Karinolov knew her well.

If Tarini carried a child, it couldn't be his, Austin thought, knowing deep in his gut that he himself had been careful. She couldn't possibly be pregnant with his child, could she?

Karinolov's laughter was rich and deep, and utterly without humanity.

"With her at my side," he said slyly, "I could have all of Byleukrainia. The Schaskylavitch name still means a lot. It would be a pleasure to call her child my own."

Austin's response was swift and visceral. He acted as a man and not as a professional. He took one hard right punch that wiped the smugness off Karinolov's face and landed the ambassador on the floor. Instantly, three bodyguards lunged, throwing Austin to the ground and drawing their weapons.

"No, guys, don't!" Bob shouted, yanking Austin's shoulder. But Austin shrugged him off.

Karinolov barked at his bodyguards in a mixture of English and Byleukrainian.

"Men, leave him alone," he said, getting up and wiping the blood from his jaw. "This American means nothing to us."

As he stepped past Austin, Karinolov let loose a rapid-fire oath in a mixture of Byleukrainian and English. His entourage seemed baffled, then visibly upset, even panicked. They hustled to the door, shouting contradictory instructions to each other in their native tongue.

"Wait a minute," Bob said, blocking the door

before Karinolov could leave. "I thought you guys were all fired up about crashing the party."

"Forget the party," Karinolov said, sneering. He narrowed his eyes at Austin. "Where is she?"

"Tarini?" Austin asked. "I have no idea. I wouldn't want to see her again if... What exactly is she to you?"

"Nothing. Everything. Nothing," Karinolov snapped, and then he issued further angry instructions to his staff. The entourage left, trotting down to the street where the limo waited.

Karinolov turned one last time to Austin.

"Next time we meet, Austin, I won't be so picky about killing an American. After all, I do have diplomatic immunity and maybe I should use it to more advantage."

"You can't."

"Oh, but I could. I could shoot you like a dog and there's not a thing this cop friend of yours could do about it."

With a shove at Bob, Ambassador Karinolov ran down the steps, past the Nigerian ceremonial guards and into the open door of his black stretch limo.

Austin stared after him.

"What was that all about?" Bob asked.

"He said something very odd," Austin said.

"What was that?"

"He was talking in Byleukrainian and I don't think he knew I was paying attention or that I know some of the language. He said he wanted the last of the Romanovs. The very last of the Romanovs. Bob, he wants Tarini."

"Why?"

"If she's pregnant with Vlad's baby, she's carrying the very last in the Romanov line," Austin said. "And Karinolov and his crowd are determined to kill every member of that family so a monarchy can never be restored to the country."

"So they want to kill her?"

"Yeah, but I'm going to get to her first."

"Tell me, buddy," Bob said. "Truthfully, what is she to you?"

"Nothing. We had an affair," Austin admitted. "But it's over."

"An affair?"

"Very brief. In December. She dumped me right after the new year."

"She dumped you?" Bob's face reflected his disbelief. No woman willingly left Austin's bed.

"Yeah, but...but it was a good thing. She's a snake."

"So now she's nothing to you?"

"Nothing at all to me personally. But she might be carrying something a lot more important than the last Romanov."

"What's that?"

"My friend's only child."

Chapter Two

Karinolov looked critically at the young woman sitting before him. She would do, for his purposes. Her hair didn't glisten quite as brilliantly as her sister's. Her mouth was not as lush and inviting. Her eyes didn't have the defiant fire of her sister's. But, then, his use for Tanya wasn't the same as for Tarini.

He had felt a deep, razor-sharp sense of betrayal when he'd heard Tarini call for Austin with her last conscious breath. He had felt such revulsion.

An American, he had thought, she was sleeping with an American. The American he hated with a passion that nearly, but not quite, matched his loathing for the pampered Romanovs.

And now, to know that she had been Vladimir's woman. His heart thrilled.

After all, it meant she was only doing her duty as a Schaskylavitch, serving her country by bringing her body to Vladimir's bed. She had done noth-

ing more than be obedient to the dictates of patri-
otism. Her mother probably explained to her the
generations of service the Schaskylavitch family
had performed for the Romanovs.

Pity that she now bore his child.

He turned his attention and his charm to the
younger sister, who sniveled on the couch.

Tanya was a bundle of nerves, just the right mixture of fear and awe and infatuation. For him.

He stood towering above her, using his height to
psychological advantage, drawing her to look up
from the impossibly low, cushioned couch. He despised the worn rugs and crowded furniture of the
Schaskylavitch apartment.

Poverty, even the genteel poverty of refugee nobility, had always repulsed him.

Still, he smiled—just enough to calm her, but not
enough to put her completely at ease.

"Where is she, Tanya?" he asked softly.

Tanya swallowed, her slender neck bobbing.

"I really, uh, can't say," she moaned, twisting a
handkerchief.

So touching, this little display of sisterly loyalty.

He crouched next to Tanya and threaded his fingers in hers. He looked at her from beneath his full
lashes. He leaned forward, close enough to kiss her,
and then backed away, as if bashful.

Tanya melted, as women always did. What was
she? Just twenty, he guessed.

"Tanya, I'm sorry if I'm so forward, I'm not…very good with women."

"But your reputation…"

He smiled crookedly, and jerked his head down, catching just the right note of boyish embarrassment.

"What people say about me!" He laughed. He was delighted to see her innocent smile. "I'm really very old-fashioned."

"You are?"

Ah, reeling her in—Karinolov had to stop himself from showing his hand. She was so trusting, so damn trusting. Not like her sister, whose heart had been forged on the refugee trail.

No, Tanya had been only a toddler when the Schaskylavitch family made it to America. She probably romanticized the homeland, romanticized his life as a soldier, as young women often did.

"Oh, yes, I'm very old-fashioned," he repeated, drawing his head closer to hers to share a confidence. "But I hope that when this time of troubles is over, you'll allow to me to…call upon you."

She glowed.

"Now, you must tell me where your sister, Tarini, is," he said, and when she pulled back, he held fast to her hand. "She got mixed up in the wrong kind of crowd. Romanov supporters are looking for her. She is in danger."

"She is safe with you?"

"Oh, yes," he said, and he suppressed his excitement as he knew that he had Tarini's whereabouts within reach. It had been his idea to charm Tanya instead of bringing in his goons. A very good idea, he congratulated himself. "What has she told you?"

"She only said that you sent Vlad back home from the mission."

"Had to be done." He looked down poignantly. "I am at heart only a soldier. I follow the orders of my leaders. What else did she say?"

"That...she was pregnant."

"And the father?" Showing concern.

"She didn't tell me. She said it was better for me not to know."

Karinolov mulled this over and then noticed Tanya seemed to be reconsidering her trust.

"You are a true patriot," he assured her. "And a good sister. But she needs protection. If Romanov supporters think she's carrying Vlad's child, they'll stop at nothing to imprison her. Where is she?"

Tanya searched his face and Karinolov thought she might see the absurdity of the lies he told. Then what would he do?

Something much more extreme than mere charm, because Tarini's location was vitally important to his country—and to himself. He willed his eyes to open wide, showing the pale blue to best advantage.

"Tanya, I want to help her."

She relented. As she gave him the address, he had to stop himself from shoving her hand away from his and running from the claustrophobic apartment.

No, no, he told himself, Tanya could turn out to be useful to him in the future.

"Even my mother doesn't know," Tanya said urgently. "She thinks Tarini is stationed in another city with the INS."

"I promise I will keep this in confidence," Karinolov assured her.

He stood to leave, murmuring other soothing, flattering words. As she walked him to the door, he sighed regretfully.

"May I return?" he asked, although the notion of coming back made him recoil.

"Of course," she replied.

Just then, the door to the apartment opened and he was face-to-face with Mrs. Schaskylavitch. Elegant even in a simple black frock, her hair had just the barest touch of gray at her widow's peak. Still as beautiful as the portrait of her which was recently found at the capital palace. She held a bag of groceries, which he reached to help with. She had permanently injured her leg in the war, he recalled, and he wondered at how she managed the stairs to the apartment.

"Allow me to help," he said.

But she leveled a stony gaze on him and he re-treated. He considered his next move carefully.

"Mrs. Schaskylavitch," he said, bowing. He held his hand out for the American handshake. She re-fused, as he knew she would. He nodded with wist-ful regret at Tanya and left the two women standing at the doorway.

At the bottom of the stairs he paused.

"Mother, how could you be so rude?" he heard Tanya exclaim.

As the door to the apartment slammed shut, he smiled. He had known Tanya would do that.

After all, she was his now.

THAT SOUND AGAIN.

Curling her long legs out from under her, Tarini sat upright on the cheap tweedy couch—alert, tense, eyes skittering across the gray shadows cast on the wall by the television screen. She had fallen asleep. Her nightmare tormented her.

The feel of a coarse hand against her cheek.

But what sound had awoken her?

Nothing. Just a cat outside in the alley.

"Tarini, you're losing it," she said.

The apartment was secure. No need for panic. But a single woman in New York heard all sorts of sounds in the night. She glanced at her watch—one o'clock in the morning.

She spooked more easily than she'd like. She

wondered why. She didn't use to be that way. She used to be a professional, used to be fearless.

In the past two months, even the cats in the alley sounded ominous in that certain hour of the night. And no amount of extra dead bolts and window bars changed that. Even keeping her own handgun cleaned and loaded at all times didn't put her at ease.

Maybe because she had never lived by herself before—a fact that would be considered odd for a twenty-eight-year-old American. But Byleukrainian women were expected to stay in their parents' home until they married and moved into their husband's family's home. And though Tarini had embraced television, baseball and fast food, she had respected the most essential customs of her culture.

Her culture didn't allow for an unmarried pregnant woman.

It was better to live in this self-imposed exile, Tarini told herself. Especially for her family, who would have been disgraced. Her mother would have been cold-shouldered by her closest friends, refused service in the tiny neighborhood shops. Her sister, just reaching marriageable age, wouldn't have been welcome in any decent home, and a man would think long and hard before being seen with any of them. At least in public.

Loose. Easy. Unvirtuous. Those and worse words

would have been used to describe the Schaskylavitch women.

Tarini could have borne it for herself—perhaps
she even deserved it—but she couldn't bear her
mother and sister being punished for her sins.

The sin of having loved so unwisely.

She had packed her bags the morning after
Vlad's abduction, leaving her address only with
Tanya, not having time to explain much before
Mama was expected back from morning mass.

"Pregnant?" Tanya had gasped. "My God,
Mama will..."

That sound. From the back of the apartment.
Again.

Tarini cocked her head.

Steps on the fire escape.

She stood, buttoning her jeans, which she had
undone because she was starting to thicken in her
middle. Cartons of Chinese food and leaky soy-
sauce packages littered the coffee table.

Slipping her feet into her sneakers, she walked
noiselessly through the kitchen and paused at the
door to the mudroom.

Had to be the guy upstairs taking out the garbage.
These yuppies didn't get home from work until ten
and they did their laundry and took out their garbage at the oddest hours. Oblivious to everything
around them while they gabbed on their cellular
phones.

That's why she had picked this apartment building—no one would notice a single woman hiding out.

She stood silent, resisting even the urge to push her blue-black hair back from her face. She listened with all her being, and counted footsteps.

There were five of them, she realized, feeling a red-hot flush springing to her chest and neck. Her heart fluttered in her throat and she gulped a breath.

Five of them.

And they weren't yuppies in dress shoes or loafers or high heels.

These visitors wore boots. Heavy boots, but brought down on each step with care. They weren't meant to be heard.

There was another sound at the bottom of the stairs—a muttered order and then a single set of brisk footsteps coming up the four flights to her back door.

If she reached for the phone, she knew she would be dead before the 911 operator even answered her call.

She quickly calculated how many steps she needed to reach the kitchen counter. On top was her purse, where she kept the gun with a seven-round clip, one in the chamber.

Eight bullets—but five intruders on the stairs.

She didn't like those odds and she started to back

away, hoping the front door of her apartment wasn't
as carefully covered as the fire escape.

A roar of gunfire from inside the mudroom. She
heard the fire-escape door kick in and the splinter-
ing of the heavy oak.

Tarini lunged for her black bag, spinning on her
heel and tearing for the front door. Toppling the
dining-room chairs behind her path. She lost precious seconds as she flipped the two dead bolts—
behind her, she heard strong boots kick the door to
the kitchen. They were gaining, and they wanted
her. Badly. Splattering gunfire like a violent rain
across her kitchen walls.

She flung open the front door. Down the stairs,
three at a time, taking four at each landing—jam-
ming her hand in her purse for the gun as she ran.
Like the set of keys that always landed at the bottom of the pile of junk, her handgun eluded her
fingertips.

Bullets tagged the wall scant inches from her
head. Shell casings clattered at her feet.

The lobby. If she could just get past the lobby.
She could escape to the cover of darkest night—
maybe even get that gun out of her purse.

Enclosed in glass, the tiny lobby had just enough
room for a pile of junk mail, a withered fern and a
folded up baby carriage. She shoved open the security door to the lobby and tripped over a toy fire
engine.

Straight into strong, muscular arms.

She screamed.

She didn't have a gun in her hand, didn't have a knife, didn't even have a set of keys to jab at his face. Still, with her arms pinned from behind by her captor's embrace, she kicked his kneecaps as hard as she could, tried to whack him with her purse and kept hollering.

She hoped one of her neighbors had sense enough to call the police.

She wasn't fighting for her life so much as the chance not to die anonymously. She knew how the Byleukrainian secret police worked—a person disappeared. Just like Vlad had done. And she had no doubt that it was Karinolov's men who had come for her.

"Tarini, damn it, stop! You're going to break my leg."

She jerked her head back and realized who was holding her. "Austin!"

The glass security door behind them shattered into a thousand little carats that skittered across the floor.

Shadowy figures rushed the stairwell.

She didn't have the luxury of telling Austin Smith to go to hell.

"Come on!" he shouted, grabbing her hand.

They ran into the deserted street, past a row of parked cars to his familiar red convertible Porsche.

He picked her up and dumped her gracelessly into the passenger bucket seat—leaping over her head to the driver's side.

With a quick kick to the accelerator, they peeled out onto the road. Her purse landed on the floor at her feet. Datebook, a tube of lipstick, sunglasses and her gun fell out. Tarini had just about decided she'd left it on the nightstand.

She scooped it up, thanked her lucky stars that she kept it loaded and looked back. Her attackers fanned out onto the road, but scattered at the approaching sound of sirens.

She didn't have a clear shot, and besides, she had made it out alive. She never wasted a shot if she wasn't sure of her target and surer still of her mortal danger.

Austin took the corner, nearly hitting a car parallel-parked in the left lane. He drove up on the deserted sidewalk and then down an alley toward a brightly lit thoroughfare.

Tarini started to breathe easier—she was alive!—then realized she had only traded a frying pan for some real fire.

"You can drop me off at the corner," she said from between gritted teeth, fighting the urge to grab the steering wheel as Austin sideswiped a garbage can, sending it flipping into the air, littering the alley behind them with paper and cans.

No way she was dying in a car wreck after surviving those goons at the apartment. If she had to, she'd jump out at the first light.

She picked up her stuff and shoved everything back into her bag, then glanced at Austin out of the corner of her eye.

He was cocky, he was arrogant, he was so damn sure of himself, but the horrible truth was, he had every right to be. He was chiseled like a marble god, had the surefooted masculine charm of a star, was wearing a tuxedo as easily as any other man wears jeans and was smarter than any man she had ever known.

And he had just saved her life.

"How did you find me?" she demanded, eyes narrowing dangerously.

"Your sister, Tanya."

"I swore her to secrecy."

"Yeah, well, you should have told her not to confide in Karinolov, either," Austin said.

Tarini gasped. "She's talked to him!"

"She believes he's a hero. I think I saw love in her eyes."

Tarini groaned. Tanya and she had always disagreed about what was best for their homeland.

"I should have told her about what happened that night at the embassy. I didn't have time. I just wanted to clear out of the apartment as fast as possible," Tarini muttered. "I only told her about..." She hesitated. She wouldn't tell him. Maybe Tanya hadn't told him, either. "Drop me off here," she said abruptly.

"No way," he said.

"Thanks for getting me out of there, but I'll just take it from here, if you don't mind."

"Don't you want to know what they wanted from you?"

She hadn't had any time to think—a glance at her watch confirmed that not more than five minutes had elapsed from awakening to the first suspicious sounds, to this bizarre late-night ride down Seventh Avenue.

"I assume Karinolov's secret police wanted to kill me because of Vlad," she said. "But why now?"

Austin gave a brief description of the confrontation at the Nigerian ambassador's party. "You've got something they want," he said, pulling to a stop at the light. The light turned green, but he put on his emergency lights and cars pulled around them.

Tarini knew now would be a good time to bolt, but she was curious.

"They want my grandma's secret recipe for *klatschkes?*" she quipped, affecting nonchalant interest while her knees were wildly shaking.

"No. They want Vlad's child."

She took it like a slap in the face. It took every ounce of willpower for her not to dissolve under his narrow-eyed gaze. He hated her. He always showed his emotions in his eyes, and where once there had been affection, was contempt. He hated her and he had every right to.

Now he knew she was pregnant and she also knew it was useless to deny it. In his eyes, she had been two-timing him.

She could tell him the whole truth, lay everything out between them. Explain it all. But then she remembered why she hadn't wanted to tell him about the pregnancy in the first place. She didn't want his obligation and his honor—she'd wanted his love. And the constancy that he wasn't capable of with women. Neither she nor her baby would benefit from Austin coming into their life then exiting again with a whim and a definite idea about how to do things. And he always had the most definite ideas about how he wanted things done.

"Vlad's child?" she said hollowly. "But what do they want with an innocent child?"

"You're carrying the last of the Romanovs," Austin answered, his mouth curling in a tight frown. "Whoever's holding Vlad isn't satisfied with just him—they want to decimate the whole line. You are pregnant?"

The question was an abrupt end to his explanation, but expected.

Tarini flushed. "Yes," she admitted.

"Was it Vlad?"

He reached out and squeezed her shoulder. It

didn't hurt, but she winced because she didn't want his touch, didn't want him to interfere with her reasoning. He backed off with a muttered apology, but she got the message. He wanted answers.

And he was who he was, her memory hadn't failed her. If he thought the baby was his, he'd stick with Tarini for the rest of his life. Not out of love, but for honor.

If he thought it was Vlad's...

"I'm waiting, Tarini," he said impatiently. "I've long since stopped caring about you dumping me or even about two-timing me, but I want to know if that's a Romanov baby you're carrying."

"And if it is?"

"If that's Vlad's baby you're carrying, you're attracting the wrong sort of crowd."

"They won't stop with tonight?"

"Lady, they're going to stop at nothing to get you," Austin answered, shaking his head. "Tonight was just the beginning."

"Do they want me dead?" Tarini tried her best to keep her voice neutral though inside she was shaking with horror.

"They'll take you dead, but I think they want you alive," Austin said. "At least, so they can publicly execute you—so there won't be any Royalists thinking there's a secret Romanov still alive. Remember—the mystery of whether they really killed

Anastasia kept the Russian Royalists going for years."

"So I'll have a chance of being led back to Vlad," she said, her mind leaping quickly ahead. "They'd want me and him together—for a final reunion—if you want to call it that."

"Correction," Austin said, in that damnable we're-doing-it-my-way voice. "*I'll* have a chance of getting back to Vlad. And I'm going to keep you away from them…for the baby's sake."

"You mean, little Vlad?"

He stared at her, a quick play of emotions flickering across his face. None of them good. She hadn't actually lied, hadn't actually said the words, "This baby is Vlad's," but she'd done enough. "Little Vlad" was all the confirmation Austin needed.

He glanced into traffic, muttered an oath as he abruptly swung the Porsche onto a side street.

"They're still on our tail," he muttered.

She shoved her hand beneath her seat, found the velvet box with Vlad's ring and slipped the diamond onto her left ring finger.

It felt heavy. She hadn't worn it since the kidnapping. But she hadn't planned on having to see Austin, to carry through the lie.

"You twisted me up so much," he said grimly, banging his head against the headrest.

"Thought you were over it," she said with a chilly quality she didn't feel.

He closed his eyes briefly, painfully, and Tarini gulped. She could tell him the truth now, this one last opportunity to clear up the confusion.

But she was bait. She knew it. She was the bait that Karinolov wanted. But only if she carried a Romanov.

So who did she lie for? The love of her life or the leader of her homeland?

"Austin, maybe I better explain—"

He jerked his head in disgust.

"Don't bother," he said dismissively. "I don't have time for explanations. You might be important to others because of some ancient monarchy crap, but you're important to me only because you're carrying the child of my best friend. No other reason, understand?"

"Austin, I—"

"Understand?" he interrupted coldly. And she glimpsed the unyielding will of iron which had made her bolt in the first place.

"Sure, I understand," she said, scrambling to recover her pride and her balance. "And that makes you nothing more than my fiancé's...employee."

She held out her hand to display the Romanov diamond as if for her enjoyment, sending a very pointed message to Austin.

He glanced in the rearview mirror, but she knew

that he had seen the ring—the sparkling five-carat gem was hard to miss.

"Good, we lost them," he said.

She pulled out the sunglasses and put them on though it was past midnight and the street glowed with the half light of the city.

Then she leaned against the headrest, tilting her chin up with just a shade of spoilt pique. "Just drive, Austin," she said with wobbly imperiousness.

Chapter Three

Tarini jerked awake and pulled off her glasses.

"What are we doing here?"

They were parked in the reserved spot in the garage beneath the San Remo, Austin's building overlooking Central Park. For a moment, she felt transported in time, to the late-night hours of their December affair.

Memories flooded her mind, memories of so many kisses.

Sometimes their kisses had been so passionate they couldn't break away long enough to go up to his apartment. Kisses that lasted all night in a gray concrete lovers' hideaway amongst the parked cars, kisses so fulfilling they were their own reward.

But it wasn't their December affair.

April was deceptively cold, some men with guns wanted her dead and there weren't any kisses left between them. And Austin wasn't sticking around. Or, at least, Tarini hoped she could ditch him again.

"Stay right here," he warned and jumped out of the Porsche. "I'll check out the apartment, see if it's safe. I'm not sure how close they are, but it's possible they'll try to get to you here. If it's safe, we'll stay here for the time being. If it's not, we'll know soon enough."

Tarini started to protest and then said nothing. She didn't have the energy to say she didn't ever want to see his apartment again, and she knew that any words would draw them into another argument. She let him go, unbuckled her seat belt and stretched her arms.

She was disoriented from a nap that couldn't have lasted more than five minutes. Her neck hurt from being contorted on the backrest. Her mind was numb with combined shock, terror and exhaustion. And her feet tingled from the pounding they had taken in the escape from her apartment.

As the security door snapped shut behind Austin, she felt the unwanted whip of fear uncoil up her spine. She had felt safe in his presence—funny to feel that way when half-a-dozen men had just broken into her apartment with automatic weapons trained on her back, she thought humorlessly.

But she knew that Austin would do everything possible to save her—even if he despised her. And she knew that he was skilled, very skilled. If there were any set of hands she should place her life in, it was his.

But she didn't want to feel that way, couldn't trust herself to depend on him. Even now. Especially now.

She slipped out of the car, stretching her legs.

Then she tried to apply logic to the situation in which she found herself.

Vlad was alive. Vlad was someplace, held by somebody—somebody with the new Byleukrainian military government.

That somebody thought she was carrying Vlad's child and they wanted her, too. Whatever else Vlad was, he wasn't, by himself, the glittering prize of total annihilation of the Romanovs.

She was. They had to kill the unborn Romanov child, too. She and her baby were in danger because some people wanted to destroy Vlad's legacy. But she was also the tool that could be used to gain Vlad's safety.

And what would Austin do? Put her somewhere safe and look for Vlad on his own. He was a loner, and since he was good—very good—he didn't think he needed anyone else.

She didn't doubt he'd go after Vlad with the same determination that he'd applied to every other job—more, since he felt for Vlad as for a brother.

But he would do it without using his most important bait—Tarini Schaskylavitch.

He was doomed to failure if he put her in hiding, but he would shield her from danger, anyway.

But she wasn't a stay-at-home-and-wait-for-the-men-to-fight-it-out kind of woman. Her pregnancy wouldn't take her out of commission, as Austin no doubt thought. She wouldn't be surprised the next time someone pulled a gun on her. What had happened at the apartment was a fluke. From now on, she'd be prepared.

She squared her jaw and put her purse over her shoulder. She walked briskly toward the heavy steel fire-escape door, picking up her pace as her resolve deepened.

She'd find Vlad, whatever it took. She'd play it safe, sure, but she wouldn't cower any longer. Her people depended on her. If she had to walk to the U.N. mission and face down Karinolov himself, she would.

Down the fire-escape stairs—not at a run, but she nonetheless kept up a quick pace. She didn't want to tire herself out, but still wanted to keep far ahead of Austin.

At the alley, she rued the fact that she hadn't a coat. Goose bumps covered her arms, and she shivered—fear or cold, it didn't matter.

She walked on the curb, craning her neck frequently, hoping for a cab. She used the solitude to formulate a plan. Couldn't go back to the apartment, probably should try to place a call to the mission, give them a little tease about her whereabouts. See how well she could draw them out. And she had to make contact with Tanya, had to set her little sister straight on what a monster Karinolov really was.

She patted the bottom of her purse, feeling the reassuring outline of the loaded gun.

Suddenly her heart went *thaddump!*

The red Porsche sidled up to her, slowing to match her pace. He looked cocky. She wished she wasn't shivering. There'd be heat in the car. She even saw a yellow down jacket flung over the passenger-side headrest. He had changed into soft jeans and a chambray button-down shirt.

Tempting. But no. She had business.

"Tarini, get in the car," he said, leaning across the passenger seat.

"Forget it. I'm a free agent. I'd thank you for saving my life back there, but you're the one who put me into danger by dealing with Karinolov tonight. So I'll just say goodbye here."

She kept walking, but the shiny red shadow stayed with her.

"You're under my protection," he said.

"Fat lot of good it's done me so far."

"I got you out of there."

"You also brought them there by shooting off your mouth at the Nigerian mission. You would have protected me a helluva lot better if you'd stayed home."

She'd hurt him with that. She didn't like doing

it, but it was necessary if she was going to get rid of him. Telling him he had put her in more danger instead of less might make him mad, plant the seeds of self-doubt. She could run with that.

But he didn't drive off in anger, didn't even look perturbed at the idea that he had let her down. Instead, he laughed, so sure of himself, so seemingly amused by her anger.

"Get in the car," he repeated.

"Look, I understand the Constitution. You have no right to make me do anything I don't want to do. Go away or I'm calling the police."

"You can't do that. You draw attention to yourself and, knowing Karinolov, he'll figure out a way to get you deported to Byleukrainia or worse."

"Maybe that's what I want."

"I know what you're thinking, but you can't bargain for Vlad if you're in a prison cell."

"So I promise not to call the cops if you promise to leave me alone."

"Get in the car," he growled.

"I don't take orders from my fiancé's underlings."

"Get in the damn car!"

She knew he wasn't used to her ignoring him. He had always chosen what restaurants they'd eat at, what movies they'd see, and if he ever thought to ask her what she wanted to do on a Sunday afternoon, she had always answered, "What would you like to do?'' Her mother's training on how a woman deferred to the man she loved had been nearly unbreakable, even for a woman as independent and strong-willed as Tarini.

If the situation weren't so desperate, it would be kind of fun to disobey him. But it wasn't fun, it was the difference between life and death for Vladimir.

"I'm not going with you!"

"I've got a nice warm jacket," Austin said enticingly. Though the days were warmer, the night was cold.

"Look, Austin, there are a few things you oughta know," she said, tossing her hair back and trying for a good dose of contempt. "I played you for a fool and I betrayed you with your best friend. Two-timed you. Strung you along. Then when I was tired of you, I threw you away like yesterday's newspaper."

"And I thought you were such a nice girl," he said laconically.

Tarini swallowed and plunged ahead. "If you can't take a hint, let me spell it out for you. Austin, I don't need you, I don't want you, and I don't give a damn about what happens to you..." And here she faltered in her barrage of carefully constructed lies. But she had to go on. "I don't care what happens to you. And while I care about Vlad, I'm not risking my life for his. I was just out for a good time. Party's over. Time for you to go home. You can find Vlad on your own. I've given up. Girl's gotta think of her future.''

His eyes narrowed and she thought she had gone too far. He eased out of the car and held out the jacket to her.

Some emotion transformed him, washed over him, changed the natural superior edge of his jaw. It was something—subtly humble yet completely powerful—she had never seen on his face before.

"I don't care, Tarini," he said grudgingly. "You're a...witch and you two-timed me and you know what? I don't care about any of that. I'm here for you and I'll sacrifice my life for you if I have to. And that's the best offer you've had all night."

She stood still, feeling more vulnerable than she had at any time since...since the night at the mission. He was offering an unconditional promise of everything. Everything but love, of course.

"Tarini, just take the jacket," he said gently, holding it out to her without coming a single step forward, as if sensing her limits. "You're freezing. We can negotiate whether we stick together—but at least stay warm while we're doing it."

She hesitated and then grabbed. The jacket felt warm and comforting. She pulled it around her shoulders, capturing his scent on it, and zipped it. It was big, way too big, but warm.

"You didn't really mean it about Vlad, did you?" he asked.

"No," she admitted. "I love him."

And she did, but not in the way Austin thought she meant.

"The other stuff I don't care about, but he deserves better," Austin said. "From both of us."

Tarini blinked back tears. He could think the worst about her, or at least nearly the worst since he hadn't swallowed the idea of abandoning Vlad. He could think the worst and it didn't stretch his credulity.

He thought she was a double-crossing, lying, two-timing, cold-blooded witch. And it didn't shock him anymore.

And she had been the one who had led him to that conclusion.

Someday, maybe after Vlad was free, she would tell him he was wrong. But for tonight, she'd have to let him hate her.

"What now?" she asked. "What do we do for Vlad?"

The featherlight lines on his forehead deepened and she knew that their troubles had gotten worse. He looked scared. And that, on Austin, wasn't something she'd ever seen before.

"They've been to my apartment," he said. "It's trashed. Karinolov must have figured out that I'd come for you—and he'll stop at nothing to find us. I say we get out of town. Together and fast."

There he was again—cocky and sure.

The vulnerability in that moment of confessing their shared love of Vlad had evaporated, but with the new understanding that he was her protector, at her service, for as long as it took. And her betrayal of him counted for nothing, at least for tonight.

It was a fantasy to think that he could forgive her, that he could forget what she had done to him. A fantasy to think she could trust him, to think she could place her life in his hands and give up the struggle inside her and forget the one that was unfolding on the streets even now.

It was a fantasy to ever think that he could have loved her. It might be a fantasy, but it was enough, she decided. At least until morning.

Silently, she got in the car and he closed the door behind her.

"I can't make it much longer," she said finally as he slid into the driver's side and started the engine. She hated the admission, but she couldn't fight her own body any longer. "I need some sleep. Only a few hours, then I'll be fine."

"I know just the place," he said confidently, and drove off.

Chapter Four

Karinolov leaned back in the plush leather armchair in the private apartment of the United Nations mission. He absently played with an onyx ring emblazoned with the Romanov crest.

The ring, and everything else in the eight-room suite on the top floor of the mission, had belonged to Vladimir Romanov. Now it was his.

It thrilled him to touch, to hold, to claim as his own everything that had once been Romanov property. Soon he would own the Romanov woman.

He spoke softly but firmly into the phone.

"Find her," he said.

"Look, I have no idea where she is."

Karinolov hated whining.

"She is with him. Find him and you'll find her. You have to know where he is."

"He hasn't contacted me."

"He will. And when he does, I want to be the first to know."

"I don't know...I don't know if I can. I love him."

"I own you. Remember? The money. Think about the money."

There was a soft groan on the other end of the line.

"I can't do this to him. He's my own..."

Loyalty. There it was again. The insufferable idiots he had to deal with!

"He won't come to any harm," Karinolov interrupted, thinking of how Austin was his to deal with. It had become personal. Karinolov was not leaving Austin to his underlings, but there was no reason to explain all of this now.

"I don't want him. He won't come to any harm. I want the girl," he said. "The girl means nothing to you—or to his ultimate safety. But she means everything to me and to my country."

Karinolov hung up without hearing out the sputtering reply. He looked at the onyx ring appreciatively and remembered that he needed to cover his tracks. He dialed again.

"Tanya?" he whispered into the phone. He carefully modulated his voice to communicate sorrow, empathy and concern. "Tanya, I didn't get to her in time. The Royalists got to her apartment first, but, luckily, she escaped. If you hear from her, you must call me immediately. I want to help her, truly I do."

AFTER THE FIRST three calls made from the phone on the nightstand, Austin wished he had the luxury of making them from a lobby phone of the Plaza Hotel. Having Tarini curled in bed with her almond-shaped eyes tracking his every move made him self-conscious.

He found himself being more jovial and light-hearted on the phone than he meant to be, more than the situation called for. But he knew she was tired enough that despair had a foothold.

He wanted to comfort her with good news—but there was none.

Phone call after phone call dug up bad news. Finding a safe house was going to be impossible. And he knew she knew how desperate her plight was.

Buddies from the State Department, from other missions and from embassy offices in Washington were uniform in their assessment. Word had gone out from the Byleukrainian military government. Karinolov wanted her. Her connection to the Romanov family made her an official "traitor" to her country.

Tarini was hot. A wanted woman. Dead but preferably alive. She was still a Byleukrainian citizen, even if she had lived in America for years, had even loyally worked with the American government as a special agent. She was still a Byleukrainian, and that country wanted her back. The military regime was determined to take her.

Anyone caught helping her risked retaliation. And there wasn't anybody who didn't understand that the retaliation would be much more severe than simply not being invited to the next Byleukrainian mission ball.

"Can't, Austin," a high-school buddy who was now a top member of the Moroccan mission replied when Austin asked him to give Tarini sanctuary for the next several days. "I've gotten word from our capital. There are enough Moroccan nationals living in Byleukrainia that—well, you get the picture. Our government couldn't put those people in danger."

Austin wanted to hold her and comfort her and remind her that he would lay down his life before any of those goons touched her.

Then he caught himself. She was the woman who had betrayed him, who had two-timed him with his best friend, who had taken his heart and thrown it away. She didn't deserve his sympathy.

Oh, he meant every word he'd said about it not mattering that she had betrayed him. It didn't matter when it came to protecting her and the baby within her and finding Vlad.

But that didn't mean he had to like her, had to give a damn about her feelings.

And after the child was born, what then?

It didn't matter, Austin thought ruefully as her eyes blinked once, twice and finally closed in sleep.

Austin called Bob Kearner, waking his friend from a sound sleep.

"Austin, where have you been, buddy?"

"Can't tell you. Won't tell you. Nothing personal."

"But you're still in the city?"

"Yeah, stuck here for now, but I've got to get Tarini out of here. Look, Bob, how bad is it on the streets?"

"There's a contract for her from Karinolov's crowd. A tidy reward for bringing her in—bonus if she's alive. Anybody can collect. Austin, buddy, if you dump her now, they might not kill you, too. I'd seriously consider the consequences of being with her right now."

Austin looked over at Tarini. Asleep, she didn't look capable of the betrayals she had wrought. Her skin was smooth and barely tinted with warm brown undertones. Her lashes were thick and dark, her hair sleek and dark. He knew it would feel warm and silky in his hands. She looked thinner than he remembered her, her cheeks more prominent, the hand that held the blanket to her shoulders seemed more delicate. She was beautiful—worse, she was bewitching.

She had been his downfall.

He wanted to touch her, to kiss her cheek and

tell her, as he used to, that he wanted her. But now his wanting was not something he felt exclusively as a physical hunger. There was a tenderness, something he had not felt with any woman…

The Romanov diamond blinked on her left hand. A five-carat wake-up call. He looked away.

"No, I can't dump her," he told Bob. "Even if she deserves it. She's pregnant."

Bob whistled. "It's Vlad's?"

"She'd have every reason to tell me it isn't his," Austin said, not trusting himself with the answer he would have given months ago—that she was too honorable to lie.

"The last of the Romanovs." Bob whistled. "Does she know that makes her a dead woman?"

"Oh, yeah, she knows the story. If she said it was anybody else's, she wouldn't have a price on her head."

"Listen, bring her here. I'll take her. She can spend the next few days with my wife."

"No, Bob, really, I don't think—"

"Come on, drop her off now. Tonight."

"No, you've got those little ballerinas to think of. I can't let you take her in. She's too damn hot."

"All right, Austin, but keep me informed. All right?"

They talked for a few more minutes, agreeing that Austin would call the next day and that Bob would make a few discreet inquiries.

They both agreed. Situation: hopeless.

Austin hung up the phone and felt the weariness he had held off for so long. He pulled off his shoulder holster, took his keys and wallet out of his jeans pocket and put them on the nightstand. Then he found the handcuffs that he kept in his back pocket.

He thought about cuffing her to the bed, remembering the panic he had felt when he'd come back from the ransacked apartment to find her missing from the parking garage, amazing himself as he listed the many different ways she was untrustworthy.

But it was a terrible thing to do to a woman, to cuff her like a criminal.

Still…

He slipped one cuff on the wrist she held up next to her head, and the other on the headboard.

There!

She wasn't going to leave him now, unless she planned to take a queen-size bed with her.

He sat on the armchair by the nightstand and put his feet up on the bed. He leaned back and tried to sleep.

Then he jerked out of his near rest. He studied Tarini, who slept unaware of her captivity. He had never known much about her—she had so carefully avoided questions about herself, her family and especially her past.

And maybe he hadn't really asked.

Their physical need for each other seemed to wipe out any chance of unwrapping the many layers of intimacy—how many times had they planned a night of theater, of dinner at a new restaurant, of a movie—and ended up in bed instead?

Besides, what little he did know about her he wasn't sure he could trust. Maybe even her desire for him had been a lie, maybe even the moan she made when she climaxed was part of an act.

He didn't torture himself replaying the memories—he had done enough of that already.

He simply remembered that she didn't like to feel trapped. He knew that emotion wasn't faked. He unlocked the cuffs without disturbing her and put them next to his wallet. He'd have to hang on to her some other way.

He carefully eased into the plush hotel bed and put his arm around her waist. Her stomach felt as flat as he remembered it—and he marveled at how little he knew about pregnancy. He had expected her to be softer, rounder, fuller. But what would he know about pregnant women?

He slipped his fingers beneath her. His own personal brand of cuffing.

She stirred and he held his breath, fearful she'd awaken and then he might have to change his tactics. But she snuggled up against him, just as she had done short months ago.

Oh, how it made him hard to feel her against him!

He wondered if this was a good idea, to be so near her. And for several minutes he cataloged her faults. There were a lot of faults, not the least of which was that she might get him killed.

But she was his only link to his friend. If Vlad didn't get through this mess alive, at least his child could live on.

This time, he promised, he wouldn't let Vlad down.

As he fell into an uneasy sleep, his hardness unrepentant but under control, he was certain that he heard her murmur his name in her sleep.

Chapter Five

Tarini opened her eyes to blinding sunlight as Austin flung open the heavy hotel-room curtains. Beyond the window came the sounds of early-morning traffic around Grand Army Plaza. The budding trees of Central Park were barely visible above the windowsill.

What ever happened to sleeping in? she wondered, shoving her head into the pillow.

And then she remembered—everything.

It was horrible to recall the night before, and yet, there was some part of her that thrilled at being with Austin again. He was here, his voice nearby humming a Mozart sonata.

Squelching a frisson of pleasure, she pulled her head up and glanced around the room. The armchair cushions looked perfectly arranged and not nearly big enough for a man of Austin's size. She jerked her head back to the other side of the bed.

He couldn't have…he wouldn't have…he didn't, did he?

If he had slept next to her, that would explain all the disturbingly erotic dreams she'd had. She had to ditch this man—but fast! Having him around was trouble.

"Breakfast time," Austin said smartly. "I got room service to bring all the major food groups. Remember, you're eating for two."

He held the tray over her head and she squirmed into an upright position. Proudly, he laid it across her lap. With a regal flourish, he took off the silver dome covering the gold-rimmed plate. He held up the heavy white linen napkin to put on her lap.

"Voila," he said. "I think, given the history of our relationship, I'm really going the extra mile for you with breakfast in bed."

Tarini looked down at the plate.

Ghastly smells. Disgusting lumps of food on the plate. A sudden roiling in her stomach. Her head felt heavy. She turned away.

"Yuck. It looks so gross. What is that stuff?"

"Scrambled eggs. Crispy bacon. Hash browns. A half grapefruit. You used to love a big breakfast."

"Get it out of here!" She leaped up, knocking the tray to the floor.

"Is this that independence stuff again?" Austin demanded. "You know, that I-don't-need-any-special-treatment-because-I'm-pregnant stuff? Or maybe the I-live-to-torture-you-Austin stuff?''

"No!" Tarini shouted over her shoulder as she headed for the bathroom. "This is the I'm-going-to-throw-up-like-a-sick-dog stuff!"

She slammed the bathroom door and was sick. Again and again. Just like every other morning since she'd found out she was pregnant. Now at the end of her first trimester, she looked forward to the morning sickness diminishing.

She knew she'd feel better again. Sometime. Probably in less than twenty minutes. The nausea and accompanying weakness would pass quickly. She would will it so.

Knock. Knock.

"Go away!" she warned darkly.

"Would you rather have oatmeal?" he said through the door.

The thought of it made her heave again.

"Okay. How about a cup of tea?"

"That's a better idea," she conceded. She washed her face—so ghostly pale—and brushed her teeth. Wanting only to crawl into bed and stay there until the nausea passed or she died—whichever came first.

When she came into the bedroom, she noted that he had cleaned up the food, moved the tray out of sight, and was holding out a comforting cup of hot tea.

"Thanks," she muttered as she took the tea and sat on the edge of the bed, trying to steady the wavering earth with her own willpower. She remembered she was wearing just a T-shirt and a pair of scanty undies.

She ignored his appraisal of her legs, feeling too bone-tired to reach for her jeans.

"Do you get sick like this every morning?" he asked.

"Yes. Don't ever try that breakfast-in-bed routine on me again."

"Is there anything else I should know?"

"What do you mean?"

"Any other things that...you know, are different?" he asked delicately.

She shook her head, overcoming her nausea to reach for her jeans.

"That's my little reminder that I'm pregnant," she said. "Otherwise, I wouldn't notice any difference. I'm not an invalid. I'm not weak or out of commission in any way. I'm just pregnant, that's all. And frankly, if you weren't hanging around, I wouldn't think about it at all."

"Have you been to a doctor?"

"Yes," Tarini said tersely, remembering the doctor's exasperation that while Tarini was scrupulous about keeping her appointments she was utterly unenthusiastic. She hadn't even watched the sonogram screen. Somehow the mothering instinct hadn't hit her. Tarini worried it might never.

"Do you have special vitamins?" Austin persisted.

Tarini slid into her jeans and zipped them up. She noted his flicker of interest—her stomach was still flat and the slim-fit jeans still fit as well as they had the day she bought them.

Maybe just a little snug.

"I take my vitamins," she said, withholding the important word *sometimes.* "Look, you seem very intrigued by all this."

"I am. Purely because I'm responsible for you now. You're carrying my best friend's child. He's not here, so I'm responsible for you."

"Well, stop that Neanderthal stuff. You make me feel like a breeding cow."

"You're carrying my best friend's child," Austin repeated. "If anything happens to Vlad, this child is his legacy."

"And what if it wasn't Vlad's child?" Tarini asked casually, slipping her feet into her sneakers. From beneath her tousled hair, she saw his look of shock and loathing.

"There was another guy?"

She was about to tell him she wasn't that kind of woman, and then remembered she was the one who had persuaded him that she was exactly *that* kind of woman in the first place. "No, I'm asking what if it was yours," Tarini said through her teeth.

"If you told me it was mine, I'd remind you I didn't want kids," Austin said coolly. "And then I'd cuff you someplace safe and go find Vlad."

"And then?"

"Then I'd take the baby, get my mom to help out and give you a tidy settlement to start a new life. You've never struck me as the domestic type."

Tarini let out a deep breath she hadn't known she'd been holding. "Glad to know you're still a real romantic," she said, relinquishing the last smidgen of guilt about lying to him. She went to the bathroom and rummaged through her purse for a comb.

"Is it?" Austin asked, following her. "Is it mine?"

"We were careful, Austin, remember?"

She shoved the bathroom door shut to foreclose any further conversation.

They had been careful. Very careful. He couldn't even known how careful.

She had made love to him because she loved him, so much that she couldn't think clearly about all that she was risking. He had done it be-cause…well, he had had lots of women and Tarini wasn't about to guess why he had made love to her. The challenge of having yet another woman in his bed would have been at the top of his list of reasons.

She had never let him know how high the stakes were for her, certain she would scare him off. He didn't know that she had been a virgin their first time together—she had affected a cool sophistication even as her fragile heart had nearly broken at the wonder and terror of making love for the very first time.

And there had been that one time, that one time when his ardor had been so great that she hadn't excused herself to take care of the precautions.

Thank God Vlad had rescued her, immediately seeing a solution to her pregnancy, a solution that would solve so many problems—personal and patriotic—all at once.

He'd provided salvation and now, even if he weren't the living symbol of all that was good and right and wonderful about her people, she would still honor her debt to him.

She had to find Vlad.

And being Austin's captive wouldn't help.

She ran the comb through her hair, swiped a brick-colored lipstick across her mouth so she'd look nearly civilized and then deposited everything in her cosmetics bag.

She would be free of Austin soon enough. She planned to ditch him at the first opportunity.

"So what's on the agenda this morning?" she called out.

She felt for her gun, checking the safety with a grazing of her fingertips. She shoved it to the bottom of her purse—didn't want him suddenly to get the bright idea of disarming her. She opened the bathroom door.

"Where are we going?" she asked.

"You are going to my parents' house," he said, with irritating emphasis on the word *you*. "I called my parents. I want you out of the line of fire."

"Aren't your parents living in England?"

Austin shook his head.

"That's just a story we float," he said. "They have a place in Connecticut. A little farm. No one knows about it because they've had to use it a few times…as a safe house for diplomats in other tight situations. They've just returned from Africa. My father has already set up a secure perimeter."

"I…I didn't know," she said, feeling hurt because he'd never brought her into his confidence before—when they were together, when he didn't have any reason not to trust her. Just one more indication of how little she had meant to him.

"If you're going to protest about being kept safe, I can take care of you some other way," he said, measuring her with his eyes.

"No," she said briskly, striding by him into the bedroom to find the jacket he had given her the night before. "You're absolutely right. It makes no sense for me to put my life in danger."

"Vlad's child's life," he corrected.

"Whatever," she said with a perfectly measured dismissive sense of pique. She had seen her opening. He'd take her to safety, run off in search of Vlad, and she'd be home free. "Just get me someplace where no one's going to shoot at me. Then you can go and do that macho thing. I don't want any part of it."

She flounced into the armchair and picked up the complimentary newspaper. She would not give him any hint of her plans to lose him.

While she scanned the hotel newspaper—an article about a mysterious gun battle on her street was buried on page ten—he put on his shoulder holster, brushed his teeth, threw some water on his face and shrugged into his green quilted aviator jacket.

As he stood ready to leave, she was dialing her mother's apartment.

"What are you doing?" he asked.

"I want to talk to my sister."

"Don't. Your sister betrayed you to Karinolov. Besides, her line could be tapped. Karinolov would zero in on us..."

"We're leaving, aren't we? What do we care if he knows where we've been? Anyhow, my sister is not a monster. She's misguided," Tarini corrected.

"And I am her only sister. I *will* talk to her and set her straight."

Austin sullenly crossed his arms over his chest.

She held the phone and listened anxiously to the rings. She hoped her mother wouldn't answer the phone. So much explaining to do.

"Hello?"

Tarini's heart flip-flopped.

"Mama?"

"Oh, my darling child Tarini, where are you?"

"I…" She glanced up at Austin's look of warning. "I can't say. Mama, where's Tanya?"

Her mother snorted in disgust. "She's with that Karinolov."

"What?"

"He took her to an early-morning mass," her mother said. "He's got Tanya thinking he's some kind of old-fashioned suitor. He brought her flowers yesterday evening."

"Talk to her for me," Tarini said. "Explain how our country really works. Doesn't she understand what our family has been through? How can she even speak to that horrible snake?"

"I can't tell her anything," her mother said. "She was raised in America. She's a free woman, twenty years old. We gave her everything to make up for…well, she doesn't remember what our country was like. Not like you. You remember."

Tarini shuddered as she recalled her early childhood on the refugee trail leading from the capital to anywhere the soldiers weren't.

"Besides," her mother added, "I'm a little afraid of him. Afraid to say anything."

Her mother afraid? Impossible to believe that the widowed Schaskylavitch matriarch would be afraid, and yet there was an unmistakable tremor in her voice.

"Mama, I'm going away for a while," Tarini said. "With Austin. Austin Smith."

She glanced up at Austin and then registered the intake of her mother's breath.

"Who is this Austin Smith?"

"He's...a friend of Vlad's."

"I believe I met him at one of Vlad's dinner parties. Where will you go?"

"To his parents' house."

"Alone?"

"Yes," Tarini replied, knowing that her mother was thinking of the consequences of an unmarried woman traveling with a man.

"I thought you were working. Tanya told me you were doing some top-secret work for the INS."

"Mama..."

She wished she had time to explain everything. She wondered if her mother would understand.

But the murderous look Austin gave her stopped her short.

"Mama, I've got to go. I love you very much.

Talk to Tanya. Persuade her to stay away from Karinolov. I'll call later.''

She hung up before her mother could protest.

"Why'd you do that?" Austin demanded. "Told her where we were going?"

"She doesn't know where your parents live. She doesn't even know who you are. When you talked to Tanya, Mama must not have been home."

"No, she wasn't home. But she could tell Karinolov that you called, that we're going to my parents' house."

"I thought the location was a big secret," Tarini said peevishly. "Besides, I'm a professional. I listened for the click. There's no tap, Austin."

Tarini swept up her things and stormed past him to the door.

"My sister may be temporarily dazzled by that charming bastard, but none of the Schaskylavitch women are traitors to the Romanov family."

Chapter Six

In chilly silence, they walked to the palm tree–lined lobby and dropped off the room key. Austin bought a coffee to go at the bar on the first floor. It was early, a quarter to nine, the final sprint to the office for most of the people who passed them on the street.

They went through Grand Army Plaza and three blocks up Fifth Avenue to a parking lot where a laconic teenager took Austin's money and gave him a receipt.

But when Austin asked for the key to the Porsche, the kid brightened.

"I was admiring your car when I got on duty this morning," he said, smiling. "Want me to bring it out for you, sir?"

"No," Austin replied curtly. "Tarini, stand right here where I can see you. I'll start the car."

"Hey, sir, can I at least see the interior?" the teen persisted. "Maybe even sit in it? Only for a minute, man. I swear, it's just that it's such a dynamite car.''

"Absolutely not. You're not touching the car. Stand here with her."

Austin walked away.

The teen looked at Tarini.

"Is he like this all the time?"

"He's a jerk to me, too," she assured him. "All the time."

Then she looked around, surveying the city blocks. Should she make a break for it now? Or was it better to stick to her original plan of being sweet—and cooperative until he left her at his parents' place?

She was confident of her skills, knowing she could escape from a farm in Connecticut so long as she didn't have Austin to contend with. They had to have cabs in Connecticut, right?

She wasn't quite as confident she could outrun Austin in the city. She walked up the gravel lot toward the car.

"Tarini, get back!" he screamed.

Annoyed, she wondered why he was on such a control trip about where she stood. She squelched her indignation, remembering that she would soon be rid of him, and walked back to the parking attendant.

Then it happened.

She felt the heat first, at the back of her head,

like a hair dryer gone ballistic. She heard sound—
a roar and then *whoosh!* and felt the shards of
busted car windows. Glass sprinkled like hail on
the concrete lot.

The parking attendant screamed and fell to the
ground. She turned her head only slightly, but
enough to see the fireball rise in the air, trailed by
a jet-black smoke cloud that spread around the lot
like octopus ink.

A sight so familiar from her childhood in war-
torn Byleukrainia, but something she had never
seen here. Here in the safety of America.

A bomb.

Austin!

Something inside snapped and all she could think
was that she had lost him before she had even had
a chance to tell him.

To tell him what? That she loved him? That she
was scared of that love? That she was just as ter-
rified of being a mother as she was of being his
woman? That she tried her best to deny that which
she feared?

She ran toward the flames, but the heat and
smoke shoved her back as firmly as a brick wall.

She heard somebody screaming and realized that
she had joined her voice to the parking attendant's.

She ran back into the black wall of smoke, swallowing her fear. She screamed Austin's name.
Coughed and choked on black smoke.

Nothing.

"Lady, he's dead!" shrieked the attendant.

Dead?

Austin, dead?

She coughed up a lungful of blistering hot air and doubled over in pain.

Suddenly, arms reached out and grabbed her. For a second she panicked, and then, joyously, she realized it was him.

Bruised, his face tracked with splintered glass and smudged with ash. Blood running from his hairline.

But he was alive.

She hugged him, long and hard. She remembered every part of his embrace, where she had once felt safe. It was there again, all his strength and all his manliness. And in his arms, everything that they were together came back in a rush of memory.

Then he pulled away. The smoke drifted skyward. Austin's eyes searched hers. Wary. Suspicious.

Neither one smiled the smile of survivors.

"Timed device," he said simply. "Thought they might try that."

He led her out of the parking lot, after first checking that the attendant was all right. Scared but all right. Austin gave the boy his cellular phone and told him to call the fire department. Behind them, the black skeleton of the Porsche burned, the smell acrid.

"Are you okay?" she asked him.

"No," he said. "But we've got to get a car. We've got to get out of here. We don't have time to wait for someone to start shooting again."

"I'm sorry about your car," she said, feeling that her words were inadequate—worse, she was talking like a complete idiot.

"The car was just transportation," he said, sagging against her for support.

"You never used to talk like that," she said, keeping up the banter to distract him from his pain—and from his momentary dependence on her.

She knew he'd rather fall to the ground and crawl than admit to needing her.

"Come to think of it, no man ever thinks his car is 'just transportation,'" she added with empty brilliance. "It must be a guy thing. Because women never think of their cars—"

He lurched forward and she thought he was going to pass out. Instead, he briefly caressed her stomach. The touch felt intimate and worshipful.

"That's more important," he said. "Right there."

She stopped trying to talk to him.

He regained his strength, leaning less heavily on her as they walked along Fifth Avenue. They heard sirens from a distance.

Tarini let Austin's arms go and he crossed the street, taking a handful of napkins from a hot-dog stand outside Central Park. He slumped down on a concrete bench partially hidden from the sidewalk by a thick, overgrown bush.

He wiped his face as best he could, grimacing only slightly as the paper raked over the glass still stuck beneath his torn skin.

The owner of the hot-dog stand didn't spare them a glance—a true New Yorker, he had seen everything.

"We've got to get you to a hospital," Tarini said.

Austin shook his head.

"We've got to get you out of town," he countered. "They want you, Tarini, and they want you dead. They might not bother with trotting you out for public consumption. They don't need you for some puppet trial in the homeland. They'll take you dead if they can't have you alive."

She shivered, survivor's instincts telling her to run, get out, find sanctuary wherever she could.

A farm in Connecticut sounded just dandy now.

But she thought of Vlad, the key to her country's salvation, who had offered her selfless salvation when she needed it.

"Austin, if you want to get out now," she said, "I can go it alone. No sense both of us going down."

"Don't talk nonsense. I told you before, you're stuck with me. Until the end. Whatever that end is."

His voice was soft—gone was the bitterness and the arrogance and the knowing everything. He had been attacked, caught by an enemy he couldn't see. He was angry...at himself.

She took a napkin from him and soaked it in a nearby water fountain.

"Here," she said as she knelt in front of him. "You're not gentle enough with yourself."

He grunted, and bit his lip as she touched him.

"How'd you know there'd be a timer?" she asked.

"Intuition. I figured they'd find the car, but might not be able to catch up with us. I opened the door, saw the mercury liquid sensor on the dash and I just rolled. I would have looked pretty stupid rolling around on the parking lot if I'd been wrong."

"Is that why you were so adamant with the parking-lot guy?"

"Yeah, do you think I'm a jerk like that all the time?"

"No," she said with a wobbly smile. "No...of course not."

"Yeah, right." Austin grimaced. "Glad to know you like me as much as I like you."

She wiped the grime away from his face, softly brushed away the slivers of glass that weren't too deeply embedded and dug into her purse for a bandage for a cut high on his cheekbone.

He stared at her like a proud, wounded animal. He didn't flinch, didn't wince, didn't cry out, complain or curse.

But she cried.

Then she leaned forward. And with featherlight tenderness, kissed the cut on his forehead.

Chapter Seven

"I guess I shouldn't have done that," Tarini said breathlessly.

He stared at her from beneath heavy lids.

"You're right," he said curtly. "You shouldn't have done that."

But he grabbed her up in his arms, shuddering as the press of their bodies tore at a bruise in his chest. He wanted her then, and he didn't care what the consequences were. Didn't care that his love for her had been destroyed. Didn't care that she was manipulating him now as surely as if she'd taken his heart in her long, thin fingers, squeezing it until it broke.

His kiss was hard and urgent—with only a moment's tenderness before he abandoned all pretense of luring her with sweetness or words of love. This was about his gratification, his needs, his physical demands—and her feelings be damned, he'd take what he wanted from her.

With a bruising press of his lips against hers, he possessed her totally, pulling at her lower lip and exploring her mouth with his tongue.

He wanted everything that kisses could be—and more.

He would satisfy himself.

But there wasn't the womanly surrender of her flesh that he remembered from long-ago December kisses. He wondered if he was hurting her. He caught himself, aware that his hands gripped her too tightly—warning himself not to crush her. Self-consciousness held him back. And yet, he was in no mood for tender kisses and sweet caresses.

The force of his hardness was as vital and sudden as when he had been a teen.

It had been too long. Too long.

And he remembered why.

He pushed her away.

"Don't jerk me around like that anymore," he said brusquely.

"You were the one who kissed me," she said pointedly, raising her head to challenge him with wide, opaque sea-green eyes. She glanced about, and he realized she was uncomfortable with the prospect of others seeing their embrace. Was it modesty? Or was she looking for an escape route?

"You enticed me," he said flatly. "Purposely enticed me." Heaven help him, she could entice him just by being alive.

How he had worked to forget her, and now, as she crouched in front of him, he couldn't stop hungering at the swell of her breasts in that T-shirt. When she tossed her head to get the hair out of her eyes, he nearly lost it.

He took a deep breath and willed himself to calm. He had to get a grip on himself if they had any chance to survive. If he had any chance of getting through this—with any of his dignity intact.

He wasn't going to get sidetracked by a bewitching temptress who was his best friend's woman. He stared at the ring on her finger. Five carats' worth of Vlad's woman.

Focus, he warned himself. She wasn't his lover—she was his ex-lover, his best friend's fiancée, a pregnant woman, and most important, a woman with a price on her head.

And it was his job—no, not a job—it was his life's meaning to get her safely reunited with the man whose child she carried. Vlad would have his hands full when Austin completed his mission, but that would be his problem.

"Get up," he said, rising to his feet.

He suppressed the ingrained chivalrous reflex to help her up. He had to show her he was immune to her charms.

She looked up at him, rejecting his command. "I think we're through, Austin," she said from beneath jet lashes. "Let's shake hands on it and part as…nearly friends, not quite enemies."

"I agree we're through, but I'm still responsible for you. I told you before, I despise you…but I'm laying down my life for you. So get up and get moving before you provide these killers with the perfect target. Or else, I'll lie down on top of you right now and wait for the bullets to fly."

"That was always your problem," she said archly. "An overactive sense of responsibility. There's another English word for it—bossy."

"It's better for you than the alternative," he countered. "At least you're alive. Come on, Tarini. I'm getting you out of here."

He shoved his hands up under her armpits and dragged her to her feet. When she whirled, he ducked. Knowing a slap was coming. It never came.

"Don't touch me again."

"Then do what I tell you to do."

"I'm not your slave."

"No, if anything, I'm yours. Because I've chosen to serve you. I'm getting you back to your fiancé so that you can be a family again, and I'm going to tear apart any man who tries to interfere with that."

"Then what was that kiss all about?"

"I don't know," Austin lied. He knew what it was. It was lust. Survivor's lust. And maybe, just maybe, he hadn't gotten her out of his system. But he added truthfully, "It will never happen again."

She stood a little closer, challenging him with her light scent and sparkling almond-shaped eyes.

"Never?" she asked.

He set his jaw determinedly. "Never," he confirmed. "Now, let's get out of here. If they put a timer in the car, they might have had surveillance on the parking lot. Even if they weren't watching, they're going to figure out pretty soon that you and I aren't dead. We have to get moving. You're going into safety and I'm heading for Byleukrainia to look for Vlad."

Tarini pointed to the drops of blood on the sidewalk at their feet.

"But you should go to a hospital."

"You have to learn to be a little more creative about ditching your men," he said, shaking his head. "No hospital. We gotta get moving. They might be anywhere."

They looked around the crowded street. Most passersby didn't give them a second glance. But any one of them could be a killer. Or anybody in the cars on the street could be holding a gun. Or someone at the window of any of the dizzyingly high skyscrapers could be a sharpshooter.

They were a target waiting for their marksman. But Austin wasn't going to wait around, and from the darting fear in Tarini's eyes he figured that she would follow him. If only for the moment.

He stepped out onto the curb, scanning the traffic for a cab. He saw one up the block and it looked empty. He whistled loudly.

"Hey, Austin, just one second."

He glanced back at her. She stood next to the hot-dog stand where they had gotten the napkins.

"Aren't you hungry?" she asked.

"No. And you can't tell me that twenty minutes ago you were throwing up at the sight of food and now..."

"I'll take three hot dogs," she said to the vendor. "And put some of that sauerkraut on them. A little more mustard, please. Those pickles look heavenly. Oh, and a couple of bags of chips."

"I said I wasn't hungry!" Austin scowled.

She gave him a blistering look. "Did I say any of this was for you?"

AFTER HANDING Tarini her purse, Bob closed the passenger-side door of his car. He held out his hand to Austin.

"Good luck, buddy, keep in touch," he said. "If you need anything, call me."

"Let me give you the number..."

Bob shook his head. "Don't tell me. Better that you don't tell me where you're going."

"I trust you," Austin protested.

Bob shook his head again. "If Karinolov comes sniffing around here, I don't want to have anything to tell him. Just call in when you need help. I'll be here."

"You're right," Austin agreed. "Better for you not to know. Thanks for the car. You're a good friend."

"Just bring my car back in one piece," Bob said.

"Sure, Bob."

He got in the driver's side, started the engine and pulled out of the station-house parking lot, waving once to his friend.

Austin would have liked to linger in Manhattan, driving in circles until he was certain that they weren't being tailed or until he had flushed someone out.

But he knew Tarini. She'd ditch him in a minute if he wasn't careful. In New York, there were a million places she could hide from him. And he wasn't sure he'd be the first man to find her if she did.

He headed for Connecticut.

"Don't you think putting me in hiding is wasting our greatest tool in finding Vlad?" she asked after a while, polishing off the last of an ice-cream cone they'd bought along the way. "After all, I'm the one who's got something Karinolov wants. A Romanov heir."

Austin shook his head. "It's what you've got that

I'm trying to protect. I won't risk putting Vlad's child in danger—Karinolov might do anything if he had you within reach again. Besides, if I have you with me, I'll put more energy into protecting you than in tracking Vlad.''

She opened her mouth and started to protest. But didn't.

She had finally come around, Austin decided, and he was fairly optimistic about the odds of her staying exactly where he put her as they finished the drive along the two-lane road leading to his parents' farm. A light spring rain blanketed the asphalt. The first crocuses and daffodils lined the streets.

The colors made him think of the bright oilcloth raincoats children wore and he wondered what this child would be like. Would Vlad's child be a boy or girl? For some reason, Austin could not imagine this baby as a girl.

Would he like football? Of course he would—and Austin had a brief daydream of teaching the little tyke how to pass and carry the ball.

Then he remembered that Vlad didn't like football—didn't like any sports, come to think of it. Vlad had always been sickly, suffering more than the average bouts with childhood diseases.

Vlad liked chess. He was excellent at strategizing, could anticipate his opponent's moves masterfully.

Austin couldn't work up a daydream about teaching a youngster chess.

Besides, what was he doing thinking about teaching Vlad's child anything? It would be Vlad's job. Vlad would train his son as he saw fit. Vlad would be there to decide if it was chess or football, wouldn't he?

Austin would see to it.

And what about the child's mother?

What role would she play in the lives of Vlad, Austin and the baby?

He glanced at the woman sitting in the passenger seat. Tarini seemed a complete stranger.

Hard to believe he had once loved her, although, of course, he had never said the words. He had never wanted to confuse lust—which he certainly felt for her—with an emotion that would make him want to promise to forsake all others for the rest of his life. His caution had been rewarded—she had played him for a fool. Thank God he hadn't put a ring on her finger or told her that he loved her.

In the past months, he had settled into regarding her as a cold, manipulative operator. And then a single, ill-advised kiss on a New York sidewalk had reignited his passion for her. The kiss had confused him, made it hard to think straight.

That's what she wants, buddy, he reminded himself. Confusion is what gives her the upper hand.

He didn't talk to her again along the drive.

His parents were expecting them but hadn't been told any details of why their son needed safety for a woman. They didn't comment on his injuries and Austin excused himself to his childhood room to shower, bandage the worst of it and change into a pair of familiar jeans he had worn in college.

His mother, who as a diplomatic wife had gracefully conquered the stickiest protocol problems, cheerfully put out a tea tray in the glass conservatory on the south side of the house. After ensuring that everyone was comfortable in the plushly cushioned rattan chairs, she chatted with seemingly random interest about gardening, the local schoolboard elections and the recipe for the layer cake she served. No one held up their end of the conversation and, in any other person, her incessant talk would have seemed self-centered.

Austin knew, however, that she was doing her job.

And doing it well.

His father, meanwhile, observed Tarini carefully, though he appeared to be utterly attentive to his cake. Tarini polished off two pieces of cake and three cups of tea without more than an occasional polite murmur in his mother's direction.

Exactly twenty minutes after their arrival, the stringent protocols of hospitality having been observed, Mrs. Smith put down her teacup. She asked—in a way that made it clear there was no answer but yes—if Tarini would care to see the guest suite where she could freshen up from the long drive.

Taking his cue as the women ascended the front staircase, the retired Honorable Ambassador Reginald Smith gruffly asked his son if he would like to see his latest pet project.

Austin followed his father down the hall to the richly paneled study.

"Here, look at this," the ambassador said, holding out his palm to Austin.

Austin peered at his father's hand. Barely visible was a copper square no larger than a pinhead.

"It's a tracer," his father said proudly. "Can be placed in an ordinary dental filling. We can keep up with someone anywhere on the globe with this."

Austin murmured his admiration, careful not to ask too many questions about his father's hobby. The ambassador had long been rumored to be a spy for the CIA. Or the NSA. Or Interpol. Austin had never asked, knowing it was not the kind of question that would be answered.

After a few minutes of explaining the technology involved in making the chip, Ambassador Smith carefully placed his treasure in a plastic bag and put it in his middle desk drawer.

"So what's with the woman?" he asked. "She looks like a Schaskylavitch."

"She is," Austin said. "And she's trouble."

"Looks like it. Be careful."

"I haven't been."

While his father puffed on his pipe, Austin outlined the events of the past few months. He knew he was repeating a lot that his father already knew about from his own contacts, but Austin wanted to be utterly thorough in making sure his father understood what was at stake.

Ambassador Smith nodded occasionally, interrupted the narrative a few times with incisive questions and stared out the window over the grass to the horses that were his newest acquisition.

Austin left out anything more than a cursory explanation of his own feelings, but he sensed his father understood that he and Tarini had been intimate and her betrayal of him had been painful.

"So what I'd like to do is leave Tarini with you," Austin said. "She's accepted the idea that she needs to be protected for the sake of the baby and I know you can take care of her. I'll head back to New York to confront Karinolov. Now that I know that Vlad is alive, I can go after him. I know I can find him."

His father remained silent for several minutes. Then he sighed. "There's only one problem with your story," the ambassador said.

And, in a sad, wistful voice, he proceeded to tell Austin the one fact that destroyed the very last remaining shred of tenderness he felt for Tarini.

TARINI FOLLOWED Mrs. Smith to the upstairs guest suite, which consisted of a cozy sitting room lined with bookcases, a bedroom done in pink and yellow chintz and a bathroom that was bigger than the living room in Tarini's mother's apartment.

Tarini had been in fancier, more ostentatious places in her role as a special agent and in the brief time she had spent as Vlad's fiancée. But no place had ever thrilled her so much.

Maybe because no place had ever felt quite so much like a home. The home of her dreams, the silly dreams she wouldn't have admitted to anyone.

She'd furtively bought decorating magazines at airports when flying in and out of Chicago when she was working for the U.S. government. She'd always left the magazines on the plane but kept in her head the pictures of a home that could be called a sanctuary.

The suite was very much like the home of her friend Toria Tryon, who had married a Byleukrainian hero, Nicky Sankovitch. Tarini felt a quick pang as she thought of the happy couple and their soon-to-be-born baby. And Nicky's little Anya, who wasn't so little anymore—nearly nine years old and as sophisticated as someone twice her age.

While Mrs. Smith talked about the house, Tarini looked around the welcoming room. Memorizing the arrangement of the glass-paperweight collection on the console table in the sitting room. Admiring the colors of the painting hanging over the sitting-room mantel. Sniffing the vanilla and sandalwood potpourri.

To a girl who had spent her childhood on the refugee trail with her mother and baby sister, this suite was heaven.

Someday, she'd have a home like this.

She promised herself that.

She closed her eyes as she snuggled into the stuffed chaise longue by the bed. At her fingertips, on a bamboo nightstand, were scholarly magazines, the latest bestseller, a vase of fresh tulips and a carafe of water. She breathed in the atmosphere of peace and serenity, barely listening as her hostess chatted on about the routine of the house. Her eyes started to close. Austin's mother was saying some-thing...about dinner at seven, and Tarini taking a much-needed nap beforehand.

"I've got some towels for you in case you want to take a shower," Mrs. Smith said as she came back into the bedroom. "And there's extra blankets in the armoire over...oh, dear."

Tarini's eyes flew open as she caught the tone of alarm in Mrs. Smith's voice.

Austin stood at the doorway, his face flushed and his jaw set hard.

His glare at Tarini was murderous.

"Mom, please go downstairs," he said softly but with enough of an edge that Mrs. Smith set the towels on the bed and walked out of the room without another word.

Austin waited until his mother had closed the door behind her. Then he sat on the bed in front of Tarini.

She felt fear uncoil within her. While Austin wasn't the kind of man who would ever physically harm a woman, Tarini gulped back the sudden panic that he might be about to make an exception.

"Austin, what...what is it?" she asked, pulling her knees up to her chest.

He lunged, slamming both hands down on either arm of the chaise. He had her pinned in before she could react, and he hadn't even laid a hand on her.

Tarini squirmed as he glowered at her with a mixture of revulsion and rage.

"What...what did I do?" she asked, looking for a means of escape and finding none.

She blinked at him. "Austin, what is it?"

"Measles," he said.

Tarini gasped. And with that one word, she knew that all that was or could be good and true and loving about her life had been destroyed.

Chapter Eight

"How did you find out?" she asked cautiously, stubbornly refusing to give in to her panic. Yet.

Vlad had told her his problem in strictest confidence—the most explosive secret of the Romanov dynasty.

And clearly all Austin could think of was his own fury.

There had to be some way to defuse the situation, she thought, wondering if he already knew whose child was in her womb. Was the truth, if he knew, what made him so angry?

Or was it her deception? Or that his closest friend had not taken him into his confidence about a matter of such importance?

"My father told me everything," he snapped. "How did you find out?"

She shrugged but her shoulders wobbled so much that the movement only highlighted her fear. Besides, Austin had her cornered so well there wasn't a lot of room for playing it cool.

"Vlad told me when he asked me to marry him. You never knew?"

But of course she knew that Austin didn't know. If he had, he never would have believed her claim to be carrying Vlad's child.

"I knew he had measles. We had it at the same time," Austin said. "We shared a room at the boarding school's infirmary. I had a mild case and was out for a week. His was worse. Far worse. But he recovered. I never knew it…never knew it made him sterile."

He said the last with a still shock on his face.

"Not many people did," Tarini said softly. "Can you imagine the scandal, the upheaval in the country? The last of the Romanovs unable to continue the line?"

"That sounds like something out of the Middle Ages."

"But Austin, in our country it would have destroyed the fragile stability we created after the Communists were thrown out of power."

Austin shook his head dismally.

"He was being groomed here in the U.N. eventually to take his place as leader of our country."

"I know, but…"

"He never would have been accepted by the people if he could not bring forth an heir. When I came to him, pregnant, he saw the solution to so many problems. His. Mine. Our country.''

He looked down at his arms straddling her and backed away. He sat on the bed and stared narrow-eyed at her.

The hours on the run showed on his face. Feath-erlight lines on the corners of his eyes. Mouth tight-ened and jaw muscles rippling beneath the flesh.

She wished she could put her arms around him and hold him as he slept. She wished she could comfort him because he felt betrayed. In so many ways.

But she wouldn't reach out to him. That kind of tenderness had gotten her nothing but trouble.

And she didn't know how much more he had figured out. How much of the truth did he know? she wondered. And how much could he guess?

As he stared at her, she still could feel the heat of his morning kiss on her lips. She knew the kiss on the Manhattan sidewalk had been more savage than love-struck—and it shamed her that she had responded. Had wanted more. Had been ready to fling away dignity for another. Right there on the crowded sidewalk.

She tilted her chin up defiantly and braced her-self. He didn't know yet. But he was going to figure it all out soon. Very soon. And she knew he wasn't going to be happy.

For now he was only concerned about his friendship with Vlad.

"I don't know why he never told me," he said wearily. "We were so close. I mean, did he think I would betray his secret?"

"No, of course not. He didn't tell you because he was embarrassed," Tarini said gently.

But Vlad had been forced to keep the secret. For his own reasons, for the preservation of his country—and for other reasons.

"Even aside from the political problem of being a Romanov who is the last of his line," Tarini explained, "he thought sterility made him seem less of a man. And you were always his ideal man. He didn't want to feel like he was less of a man than you."

Austin looked up sharply. "What do you mean—ideal man?"

"Oh, Austin, you have to know he thought of you as the perfect man. Handsome. Strong. Virile. Confident. Sure of himself. Attractive to women."

She had said the words without thinking—it was the truth, after all. But as their eyes met, his flashing a gray, merciless blue, Tarini knew she had made a mistake. He thought she was manipulating him again, flattering him to sidetrack the coming storm of anger at her lies.

"Who is this child's father?" Austin snarled.

"Who do you think?" she countered, offended

by the implied slur he was making upon her character.

"I'm asking you," Austin persisted. "Who's the father?"

"And I'm telling you that the answer is pretty plain," Tarini said just as stubbornly. "But I'll spell it out for you. You're this baby's father. I was with you and no one else."

"Yeah, right. It wasn't Karinolov?"

Suddenly she felt a blinding fury, coloring everything in her sight bloodred. "Karinolov? How could you even say that?"

"Before I lost consciousness, in the mission that night, I saw how he touched you. Maybe you returned the feelings…"

"I'd never met the man before."

"Then who is it?"

"Austin, I've never made love to another man besides you," and when she saw the disbelief, she blurted out, "I was a virgin!"

His steel-blue eyes flashed with an unspeakable combination of rage and disgust and—could she be seeing things?—pity.

Tarini's heart leaped into her throat. She hadn't meant to tell him about being a virgin. Had never meant for him to know. When they'd been together, she hadn't told him because she didn't want him to feel obligation to her beyond love and didn't want to lose him if he knew she wasn't as sophisticated as she seemed.

Now she didn't want him to know such a personal thing about her, didn't want him to know he'd had any influence in her life. But she had said it impulsively, defending herself against his obvious conviction that she was promiscuous.

He stared at her long and hard. And then laughed. Laughed as if she had just told him the most amusing story he had heard in years.

"I was a virgin!" she said in a raised voice.

He sobered. "Tarini, I won't even call you a liar because I think you can't tell the difference between the truth and your lies anymore."

She slapped him, catching his cheek with the full flatness of her hand. She gasped in horror as the skin broke on a cut to his cheek he had taken in this morning's explosion.

He caught her wrist and narrowed his gaze. She knew he could hurt her if he wanted, could squeeze her wrist until the bone snapped. She knew it was only his sense of honor that stopped him, that held him in check. Because right then, the animal core of him wanted to pay back her assault.

She prayed for his mercy, but kept her eyes defiantly wide open.

"I'll warn you once, Tarini. You might be a woman but I'm reaching my limit."

He shoved her away as if she were a snake.

She slumped back into her chair, rubbing the red welt he had left on her wrist.

"I can't believe you were a virgin, but I'm willing to concede this child is mine," Austin said. "But why didn't you tell me?"

"I was scared."

"Scared be damned! This is the deepest betrayal a woman can commit against a man. Two-timing me was nothing compared to this," he said, rubbing the wound she had inflicted on his face. "Wait a minute—you weren't two-timing me at all. You were never with Vlad, were you?"

"No, I wasn't."

"But you went to him with my child instead of coming to me," Austin said.

"I'm sorry. I was wrong."

"Wrong? *Wrong* is hardly a strong enough word."

"I said I was sorry. I thought you would react badly. There was one time, one time only that I didn't...that we were so urgent that I didn't take the precautions I should have. I thought you would blame me, think I was trying to trap you."

"Why didn't Vlad tell me or make you tell me?"

"Because I told him that if he breathed a word to you, I'd run, I'd leave, I'd disappear. And he hoped that one day I would agree to tell you. And that someday I would also...come to love him. Love him in a romantic way, that is."

"And until you got around to making that decision, you two would raise my child as your own in a sham marriage?" he demanded, disbelief washing over his face.

"Yes, that was our plan."

"Austin Smith's child raised as a Romanov? I mean, I'd expect Vlad to raise a child of mine if I were dead—but I'm still alive, Tarini, very much alive."

She could feel his hurt and fury radiating from him, and without meaning to, she sympathized. "He never liked the idea of lying to you," she explained. "I never did, either. But I knew you didn't want kids and you never talked about a future for the two of us. You made clear you weren't that kind of guy. You didn't want a wife and you certainly didn't want kids."

Austin slammed his fist against the headboard. "Of course I didn't want kids," he shouted. "Not many men have that longing the way women seem to. And if you had come to me, I would have been upset. No doubt about it."

"See? You prove my point."

"No, I don't prove anything. I would have complained and ranted and raved for the first twenty minutes. I don't have the kind of job, the kind of life, the kind of personality that makes allowances for a child. I might have said things in anger that you wouldn't have liked. I might have sounded like

I didn't want this child. And then—damn it. Then, Tarini, I would feel exactly like I feel now."

"Which is?"

He slumped his shoulders and shook his head. "I'm a father," he said with a touch of wonder. "You're going to have my baby. And I'm going to be a father. That's how I feel, Tarini. Can't you have any sympathy for a man who's just found out he's going to be a dad?"

For one blinding instant, she thought he would forgive her. He leaned forward with just the briefest flash of tenderness but then, just as his hand touched hers, he backed off to stare at her with undisguised suspicion.

"Why did you let me believe this is Vlad's baby when Karinolov went after you? I mean, it's a very simple matter, Tarini. If you're carrying my baby, Karinolov doesn't care about you. Why didn't you just tell me?"

"I want to find Vlad," Tarini said, lifting her chin defiantly.

"Using my child as bait?"

"I never meant to tell you about the baby."

Austin growled in frustration.

"I...don't want you taking over my life," Tarini continued haltingly. "You're the kind of man who doesn't let a woman make her own decisions."

"You're not going to make your own decisions as long as you're carrying my baby," Austin announced. "Because your decisions are utterly wrong."

"That's exactly the kind of..."

"Tarini, admit it. You're wrong."

"...pigheaded..."

"You've screwed up—"

"...chauvinistic..."

"Screwed up big time, Tarini."

She looked down at the carpet. He was right, but it was so hard to confess to him. Besides, hadn't he made some mistakes, too?

"Now I've got to persuade Karinolov to call off his dogs because you're carrying my baby," Austin said in that infuriatingly take-charge way.

"And what about me?"

"You're staying right here. Knit some booties. Crochet a baby blanket. Have my mom teach you to cook. Do something useful. And Tarini?"

"Yes?"

"Try, really try, not to make matters worse."

"I won't put up with this," she said, rising.

He pushed her back into the chaise.

"You've probably made it ten times more difficult to find Vlad by lying about the father of this baby."

Tarini shook her head as she recognized the truth.

"You've screwed up," he repeated. "Don't make it worse by disobeying me."

"I'm not yours to order around."

"Wrong, Tarini. You're mine now and you're going to do exactly what I tell you to do until after the baby's born…"

He stared at her.

"And after the baby's born?" Tarini challenged.

"You'll still do what I tell you to do," Austin said. "For at least the next twenty years."

"And if I don't agree to this?"

"There's no agreeing or disagreeing. There's just doing it."

Chapter Nine

Austin, exhausted and defeated, took another blindingly hot shower to ease the pain in his shoulder and then he rebandaged the worst of his cuts. He settled his injured body on the bed.

He forced himself to sleep, packing into an hour's rest the rejuvenation that would have to carry him through the next critical hours.

He didn't speak to Tarini, but was aware of her sitting in the next room. He could only hope that she understood that he was a man with a mission to complete and then he was hers.

Reluctantly hers.

He wasn't happy about having a child. It wasn't something he had wanted, planned on or had ever cared about.

But in the time it took him to drive from New York to the Connecticut farm, he had become so sure of his allegiance to this child as to his family, Vlad and his country. The only difference now was that he had found out the child he had pledged his life to was his own.

And he would protect Tarini's life, because her life meant his child's life. He would do whatever it took to ensure her safety, the safety of his child. If he had to go down on his knees before Karinolov, he would. But that didn't mean he had to like her.

He made that point to Tarini when he was ready to leave. He gave her a few instructions, as well. "Remember. You're staying here. When I get back from New York, I want to find you here. Right in this room. Preferably in this exact chair. Do you understand me, Tarini?"

She made a tiny pout with her mouth, the same pout that once would have made him hard with animal lust. Now it annoyed him. She looked up from the letter she was writing to her friend Toria.

"Yes, my lord and master," she said, blinking at him.

He swore under his breath.

"Tarini, I'm damn serious. If I don't find you here when I get back, I'm going to track you down and make your life miserable forever. If I find you here, on the other hand, there's a chance—just a chance—I'll be only mildly irritating for the rest of our lives."

She went back to her letter writing.

"And which alternative is worse?"

He swore again. "Tarini, just promise me you'll be here."

She must have heard the naked concern. "All right," she conceded. "Cross my heart and hope to die."

He let out a deep breath. He decided he wouldn't ask her if she was crossing her fingers under the desk.

"Good. I'll be back by tomorrow. And if I fail..." He felt his dignity slipping away like sand through his fingers. "Tarini, please, do me one favor."

She narrowed her eyes, and he guessed she was trying to figure out if he was laying a trap for her.

"What favor?"

"Please, raise him to know me," Austin said, his voice cracking. "Tell him I would have loved him and that I wished with all my heart to be a real dad to him. Raise him as a Mets fan. Send him to my Sensei in Brooklyn two nights a week when he turns six. Don't let him get any tattoos until he's old enough not to regret it."

"What if this baby is a girl?"

Austin hadn't thought of that. "Do the same thing," he said. "And, please, Tarini, don't tell any child of mine that I was a complete jerk, all right?"

She startled at his request. But he had gotten through to her. It would have to be enough.

The thought of a child of his being raised never

to know him was torture enough without thinking of Tarini bad-mouthing him every step of the way.

"So I'm going to explain to the baby that you're not a complete jerk," she said, the twinkle in her eyes leaving no doubt that she was teasing. "Wouldn't that require me to lie?"

Austin looked her up and down. He was in no mood to be cheered up. "You're good at lying," he said curtly.

Without another word, he left, closing the sitting-room door quietly behind him.

He would have wanted to kiss her, to hold her, to breathe in her scent for possibly the last time— and he hated himself for wanting her even now.

He accepted a sandwich from his mother, who stared at him with a worried expression but didn't ask any questions. His father promised they'd take care of Tarini and told him to be careful.

"Whose child is it?" the ambassador asked when his wife was out of earshot.

"She says me."

"Not Karinolov?"

Austin regarded his father thoughtfully. "Is it possible?"

"I met him when I was posted in Moscow," the ambassador recalled. "He's from peasant stock, but he was acquainted with the Shaskylavitch family. Would have given anything to be part of their mi-lieu. He's about fifteen years older than she is.

She's beautiful and charming and a member of nobility. Why wouldn't he want her?''

"She says the baby's mine," Austin said abruptly. "I have to do what's right. Protect her, protect that child and find my friend."

"Are you sure it's yours?"

"Not positive. But it's possible."

The ambassador shook his head. "She lied about Vlad."

"She lied for a reason," Austin said, uncomfortable with having to defend her to his father.

"Look," the ambassador said, "I know you have to go and I know that you believe honor lies in following the law. But Karinolov doesn't play by anybody's rules. Even the rules of honorable men. He's a peasant who's fought against what he thinks of as the injustices of the upper class. He doesn't care about honor and law and tradition."

"Upholding the law of nations is what you've built your life on," Austin said. "You can't tell me now that you'd want me to break the law."

"There have always been Karinolovs in the world," the ambassador said sadly. "And the law sometimes can't reach them—an honorable man does what is right, and sometimes right isn't found in the strict letter of the law."

"And?"

"You might have to choose between what is right and what is lawful—I want you to know I understand if you choose what is right instead of what is strictly legal.''

Austin was surprised by his father's admission that he himself had reluctantly come to.

He promised his father that he'd be careful—and that he'd be back.

He patted the gun in his shoulder holster and wondered grimly if he'd have to use it.

AUSTIN WAS RIGHT, Tarini thought gloomily as she watched him drive his friend's Chevy down the tree-lined driveway, she had screwed up big time.

She hadn't counted on Austin finding out the truth. And the truth now made what was already a terrible situation—Vlad's abduction—into a complete and utter disaster.

In the best of all possible outcomes, Austin would gain her safety and Vlad's freedom. But she knew enough about Karinolov's reputation—he'd exact a humiliating price from Austin. A price that Austin would turn around and extract from her. She'd be at odds with Austin for the rest of her life.

Austin would rule her and their child with an iron fist. And that was if things turned out really well.

She finished her letter to Toria—a letter that revealed nothing of her own situation but still communicated her warmth for the woman whose marriage and husband Tarini had saved. Nicky had been a captive of extremists and Tarini's quick thinking and sureness with a gun had set him free. Later, she had worked to procure the green card that kept Nicky in America.

She only wished she could have what Toria had—for herself. A husband. A son soon to be born. A stepdaughter who idolized her. And, most of all, a home. Which was nothing more than all those singular elements swirled together and sprinkled with the magic dust of love.

Instead, she had Austin.

The most horrible, wrenching part of this future was that she loved him.

She had thought that a couple of months apart from him would have worked. She had thought that she was cured. But she wasn't cured.

If anything, the time apart had only increased her appreciation of him. Those eyes were even deeper and clearer than she remembered. His hair more golden than she recalled. The kisses more brutal, but as dazzlingly potent as ever.

And his abrasiveness?—well, she understood him, understood that he was a strong man with strong appetites, strong opinions and a history of others relying on his strength.

And, worst of all, she wanted him to take her into his arms, into his bed. But that didn't mean that she had to be happy about it. She wasn't going to let him take over her life. She hadn't lived through the turbulence of Byleukrainia's civil war to be some man's slave.

Even if that man was Austin Smith.

She slipped on the jacket he had given her and pulled everything together in her purse. Then she took a deep breath, wondering how she was going to explain to the Smiths that she was leaving against their son's express orders. She wondered if she should have them call a cab or ask for directions to the nearest bus stop.

She knew she had promised to stay, but she had to leave to get her sister out of Karinolov's grasp.

She had a brief, repulsive memory of Karinolov's obvious sexual interest in her. She thought of Tanya, young and impressionable, who would take his snakelike manipulation for charm and his lies for sincere feeling. It would disgust Tarini to even speak to him again. But she'd do it.

She put her hand on the doorknob.

It didn't give.

Oh, this was too much, she thought, fighting the tremor of panic. She never liked to be trapped. It made her crazy.

She put a hand to her throat, feeling the choking sensation.

She tested the knob again. She dug a bobby pin out of her bag and tried to jimmy the lock.

She swore quietly, using a few choice words from her native language that her mother wouldn't know she even understood. And every one of those words were directed at Austin.

"So this is how it's going to be," she said. "A lifetime of imprisonment for the crime of having fallen in love with you."

She tested the doorknob one last fruitless time.

Now she knew there was nothing left of love in Austin's heart. Because love would have told him what he now had ignored.

She couldn't be trapped.

Chapter Ten

Swallowing her panic and her anger at Austin, she broke open the window lock, sliding the sash up just enough for her to squeeze through. She crawled onto the roof of the back porch, dragging her purse behind her.

And then carefully—very carefully—Tarini eased the window shut.

Fighting the slide of her sneakers' slippery bottoms, she rolled over the roof's edge. For several moments, she hung from the gutters over the grass and hosta border. When she dropped to the ground, she splattered mud all over herself and her feet tingled with pain, but otherwise her escape was without incident.

Then she looked out across the Connecticut woods and wondered which way was New York City.

In all the time she had spent in America, she had only seen its cities. New York had been her home.

Washington a place for occasional meetings with high-level government officials. Chicago a mass of skyscrapers and brownstones where she had been posted for two years working on immigration cases until her mother decided that Tarini was taking a chance with her reputation by living alone and far from home.

Then Tarini had taken the "safe" job at the mission, where she had met Austin—a definite minus in the reputation-building department had anyone known of their illicit relationship.

She stood in the Smiths' apple orchard and tried to get her bearings. The forest looked so forbidding. But then the skills so long forgotten, the ones that had helped her and her family while they were on the run in her native land, came back to her.

She sniffed the air, and decided there was water to the north. She noticed a bird flying to its nest with a prize piece of litter and figured that to the east was the town she and Austin had passed on the way up from New York. She slung her purse over her shoulder, tested her feet for pain from the fall from the roof and measured the hours until sunset by the angle of the shadows from the trees.

Tarini figured she had only an hour before the Smiths discovered she wasn't there for dinner. They'd come looking for her and she was sure that if Austin had been careful enough to lock the door, he had been careful enough to leave strict instructions that they should prevent her from leaving. He probably told them she'd try to run and trusted them to find her and bring her back.

Tarini didn't underestimate Ambassador Smith's tracking abilities. When she'd passed his first-floor study, its door ajar, she had noticed a sophisticated map spread across one wall, world-class radio equipment and a glass-enclosed arsenal of antique weapons. She wondered if he was one of the many CIA operatives who work their entire lives cloaked in the anonymity and respect of a diplomatic career.

In any event, while he was a very nice man and considered a hero to many for his selfless work evacuating refugees from certain Eastern European countries, Tarini didn't want to be at odds with him for disobeying his son's instructions.

She walked into the protection of the trees and thought carefully. Austin's father would figure she'd head for the village—that was, after all, the easiest way to get back to civilization.

But there was no way she'd reach the village before sunset. So if she headed east, Ambassador Smith would discover her absence before she had made it to relative safety.

She'd head west, for the river.

The going was rough but exhilarating. Tarini was flexing muscles and stretching her endurance in ways that she hadn't for so long. Her senses sharpened as she climbed the rocks to the river's embankment and then followed the river. She'd soon be off the Smith property altogether.

But going beyond their property line wouldn't give her the option of slacking off. She pushed herself to make good time, promising herself that she would use the first pay phone she saw to call her sister.

Maybe she'd be a step or two behind Austin in reaching Karinolov, maybe he'd already be in New York. But she also figured him to be such a control freak that when his parents alerted him that she had escaped, he'd backtrack to Connecticut. She'd beat him to Karinolov—of that she was certain.

A twig snapped behind her. Startled, she turned her head toward the embankment, but could make nothing out. The sun was dipping lower and lower over the water—nightfall would come soon and with it chilly temperatures. Tarini was glad she had brought Austin's quilted jacket but wished she had scavenged some warmer clothes from his parents' guest closet. She could see the lights ahead—perhaps a private home, a hotel or maybe even a town.

Whatever it was, it was a welcome sight, and only a few miles more.

A rain of pebbles from the top of the embankment splashed into the water next to her feet.

Tarini stopped, feeling fear slither up her spine. She swallowed and forced herself to take three deep, relaxing breaths while she concentrated on the sounds, the sights and the smells.

Someone was near, within a few yards of her. Whatever it was, it wasn't animal. The forest animals had gone quiet. The ducks had swum far from the shore. The scent of human sweat drifted to her.

She could run for it, but she knew she didn't have the stamina to reach the lights ahead. She mentally counted the rounds in the gun that she slid from her purse.

Seven loaded in the clip, and an extra one in the gun's chamber. She reached into her purse and flicked the safety.

"Ambassador Smith?" she gulped and asked hopefully. If it was Austin's father, she'd give up gracefully.

She stood closer to the embankment.

She fingered the handgun cautiously. Knowing she'd feel like a fool if it was Ambassador Smith standing above her.

Then she saw a red dot at her feet, on the new grass, brilliantly contrasted to the dark. She swallowed hard. Whoever it was had a LaserClip on his weapon, casting a beam of light in search of his target. Once that laser locked on to her body, she was as good as dead.

The red dot moved on, casting an unnatural glow on the damp, dark grass. Searching for its target. Circling back toward her. She held absolutely still.

Silence.

She thought she saw a shadow waver near a clump of pine trees. The sun was gone and it was nearly impossible to tell.

Her stomach tightened. She tried one last time. Praying that her judgment was wrong.

"Ambassador, I'm sorry. I was very angry that Austin locked me in the room and I wanted to leave, but I'm sure we can come to an understanding…"

The blow to her head was sharp and hard and totally unexpected. But the assault didn't end there. Flinging her to the ground, her attacker rammed her head against the gravel at the river's edge. Again and again, until the gritty rocks were dark with her blood.

He grunted and grabbed a handful of her hair, struggling to drag her farther into the water. Lurching forward, he held her head down. She willed herself not to breathe, and then, powerful instinct revolted and she sucked mud and water back into her lungs.

She squandered her strength on ineffective kicks, flinging up sludge until her legs felt like concrete. Coughing and throwing up water, mud, soaked grasses and bile. She rolled the battle back to the rocks, lurching away from the deadly water.

She screamed once when her attacker lost his grip on her. Uttering a harsh Byleukrainian oath, he grabbed and threw her down, his boot crunching her neck. He brought the nub of a silencer against her head, and Tarini squeezed her eyes shut.

Flailing her arms helplessly at the gun she'd dropped, she gasped out a final, impotent scream for help.

The bullet would come.

And then she felt it.

A tiny flutter in her stomach. Whisper-soft and barely there. But it was her baby. Her little baby. The pregnancy she had wanted to ignore for so long had chosen just this moment to announce, "I am here." A moment of miracle and wonder that any other mother would have had the luxury to appreciate.

With a superhuman strength she didn't know she possessed and an animal growl that came from deep within her, Tarini rolled backward. She shoved her assailant into the gravel, lunged for the gun, fumbled and was tackled to the ground.

He slurred her and ran the silencer's edge up to her forehead.

Tarini thought of her child within her.

"Austin, forgive me," she whispered. "I loved you."

There was the roar of gunfire and then blood everywhere—wet, hot and sticky.

AUSTIN HEARD the news on the car radio and though the report was vague and lacking in every detail that he would have wanted to know, Austin could fit the pieces together as easily as a child's jigsaw puzzle.

The liaison officer for the Byleukrainian United Mission, on a nature hike, had been shot to death on the Smith farm by Tarini Schaskylavitch. The reporter said a search for Tarini was under way.

"Damn it, Tarini!" he shouted and pounded the dashboard of Bob's Chevy. Concern for her warred with fury that she had willfully disobeyed him. "How do you always manage to get yourself into trouble!"

He searched for an exit ramp, in seconds pulling to a stop on the frontage road. He used the cellular phone to punch in the number to the private line in his father's office, knowing it would be the only "safe" line available.

"The authorities are all over the place," the ambassador confirmed. "They sent down some guys from the State Department. The Byleukrainians are up in arms. They brought in a chargé d'affaires from their D.C. embassy. But, hand it to your mother, she's got everybody drinking tea in the sitting room. She runs a tight ship, er, parlor."

"What was that guy doing on our property anyhow?"

The ambassador sighed.

"Oh, they're floating a wonderful story about him being a nature freak who likes to collect botany samples. And they've got a second aide who claims he saw Tarini fire the gun. Karinolov claims Tarini stalked the man because of a dispute over politics. But face facts, Austin. He's a hit man sent from Karinolov's mission and Karinolov knows the guy must have found her. He is already demanding that she be turned over to him personally or to the ambassador in Washington. That means deportation."

"Will the State Department hand her over?"

"You bet they will. She's still a Byleukrainian citizen, Austin, and officially is a member of Karinolov's staff. There's no reason to protect her. She has gotten herself into a real jam now."

"The woman is trouble," Austin said in wonder and frustration. "Dad, if she'd just done as I told her, none of this would have happened. Karinolov's men might have still tried something, but you would have taken care of it. She's trouble, through and through."

"She might be trouble, son. But she's your trouble. And I think she's alive. Out there somewhere. The dead man's gun never fired."

"She's a survivor, Dad. If she managed to get out from under that goon, she'll make it."

"She'll need your help. Find her, son, and bring her back here. We can hide her. Go through the back pathway. It's the only way she's going to be safe. Nobody else can give her sanctuary."

Austin felt a saltiness in his eyes and couldn't speak. But inside, he felt the promise he made.

He would find her.

"All right, Dad. I will."

Ambassador Smith deftly turned the conversation to an analysis of the disaster at hand. Karinolov had sent the liaison officer to kill Tarini—he must have kept a very good tail on Tarini and Austin when they drove up from New York or maybe Karinolov found out about the Smith farm from other sources.

In any event, Tarini had killed in self-defense and now was out there, somewhere in the cold Connecticut night.

If she wasn't at the bottom of the even colder river.

The two men agreed that the ambassador would do everything in his power to keep the investigating officers on the property—preferably in the sitting room with teacups and saucers in hand—and the ambassador would issue a brief, completely uninformative statement to the reporters who were converging outside the farmhouse.

His father reviewed directions on how to slip unnoticed up the back pathway to the house, cautioning Austin twice that Tarini wouldn't be safer anywhere else on earth.

As the two men finished talking, the ambassador

pleaded with his son to be careful. Austin asked his father to convey his love to his mother, he hung up and headed back to Connecticut.

He flipped on the car radio, turning the dial until he got an all-news station. The details were beginning to be made public.

Tarini couldn't get far. If he didn't find her, and fast, he would have failed her, as he had failed Vlad.

Where was she? he demanded of himself as he sped along the highway.

The body had been found a half mile from the river town of Farmdale. She must have gone there. But there had been blood everywhere—how had she managed to get more than a block into town without attracting a lot of attention? And where would she go from Farmdale? Wouldn't somebody have turned her in?

He mulled over the possibilities, knowing they were the same possibilities that a hundred officers were now considering.

Bus stations would be searched, cabdrivers interviewed, train schedules checked, beat cops sent door-to-door to ask questions, and roadblocks would be set up on anything wider than a bike path. Tarini had to know that she couldn't just walk away.

And then he gasped. Of course she knew she couldn't walk. Not east toward Farmdale. She wasn't an idiot. In fact, she was the smartest woman he knew.

Tarini had an iron will that would motivate her to do whatever was necessary to survive, he was certain of it.

Austin pulled over to the shoulder and turned off the engine. Where was she? he asked himself again.

Anybody in her shoes would have headed for the town—but that would have been lunacy, like walking into the police station and holding her hands out to be cuffed. No, he decided, she didn't go there.

She did something more complicated. What was it? He had to get into her mind. Even if he thought she was a lying, no-good, devious, manipulative woman.

When he was finished thinking, he switched on the ignition and headed away from his family's farm. Away from Farmdale, away from the dragnet.

He'd find her upriver, west, far from where her pursuers would flounder. Of that he was sure.

As he drove, he realized he had found an unbearable tenderness toward her. He loved her. Oh, how it cost him to admit it—even to himself—but he loved her. He just hoped he could shake that feeling later, after he got her out of this disaster.

But something much more urgent consumed him.

How had Karinolov known where to find her?

Chapter Eleven

"Tarini? Tarini, it's me, Austin. Come out. It's safe. I'm not even angry about your running away." All right, maybe just a little, Austin thought. But he didn't have time for anger or even annoyance.

Seven times he'd parked the car in bramble and brush—and had searched and then given up, driving farther and farther north.

Calling for her in a voice he knew grew increasingly tense with only the ducks to squawk and complain at his intrusion, he searched for anything that would tell him she had passed this way.

But there was nothing. No footprints, no drops of blood on the underbrush, no telltale threads snagged from her clothes by the thorny bushes.

Nothing.

He had either misjudged her flight or she was profoundly talented at covering her trail.

And though his love for her made him ardently hope the second conclusion was possible, he was reluctantly forced to acknowledge that the first conclusion—that he had misjudged—was correct.

Maybe she was already in the hands of the authorities, back many miles. Maybe she was already on her way to Byleukrainia—without his ever having had a chance to say goodbye. Maybe she had drowned in the muddy river and her body was floating toward the ocean...

She couldn't possibly have come this far, he thought, calculating that Tarini would have had to cover four miles an hour through the underbrush and forest and muddy shores, all without leaving a single hint of her passing.

A pro—a very skilled one—might be able to do it, but a pregnant woman in a pair of sneakers? What had he been thinking?

"Tarini?"

He stood in the silence of the woods. Nothing. A hum from the highway a half mile off, the gentle lap of the water on the shore. He wondered about his bright idea of trying to think like her. She wasn't here. He hadn't known her, hadn't been able to get into her head at all.

And maybe he had never really known her. Or how she thought. Maybe he had never been as close to her as he remembered.

Shouldn't be surprising—that's how most of his intimacies with women had been—physical, hot, pleasurable for both parties, but not intimate.

But he had thought his relationship with Tarini was different. It wasn't.

And he should have learned his lesson the day she dumped him. He should have known when she put his best friend's ring on her finger. Why couldn't he have learned his lesson?

After Tarini, he should have forgotten her, moved as far away from her as the planet allowed, found himself a nice blonde who was more... cooperative.

But, of course, Tarini had his child.

And also his heart.

"Listen, Tarini, I'm sorry about locking you up," he said aloud, pleading with the fates one more time that he find her. "You can't go running right into danger anymore. You can't just think of yourself. You have the baby to consider, and that baby—"

He heard a rustle in the trees that wasn't squirrel or deer. He pulled his hand back to his shoulder holster as he suddenly alerted—could it be possible that Tarini's attackers were out there?

Karinolov had one man down, but he could have sent others. They'd be fools to do anything with the Connecticut state trooper, the ATF, the FBI and the State Department covering them. But then again, some—if not all—of Karinolov's men would be covered by diplomatic immunity.

And Karinolov regarded his diplomatic immunity as some kind of open-season hunting license.

He heard a twig snap, and he whipped his head around and saw a glimpse of white under a jagged ledge of rock. The thin shoulders. The blue-black hair.

And the blood. Streaks of it all over her shirt, her jeans and the jacket he had given her.

He charged into the brush.

"Tarini!"

She crouched partially hidden under the ledge. He tugged at her, and a wild, convulsive shudder ran through her body as he pulled her into his arms. The blood was dry. He shoved his hands up under her shirt, feeling the clammy, but mercifully unbroken skin. She hadn't been shot.

But she was in shock.

He yanked off his jacket and wrapped it around her.

"It's all right, Tarini, I'm getting you out of here."

She started to cry—big rushing sobs.

"It's all right to cry," he said soothingly, though it looked as if she already knew that. "It's okay. You've been through a lot. It's all right to just plain be scared."

"I killed a man," she said through her tears.

"I know," he murmured, drinking in the feel of her in his arms. She was alive! And the joy of it crowded out every other emotion. Even the sensible ones like fear of Karinolov and uncertainty about his next move. "I know you killed him, Tarini, but you had to do it. It'll be all right."

She pushed his comforting arms away.

"Austin, I'm a pro," she reminded him, roughly swiping the tears from her cheeks. "And I've been in wartime conditions. I didn't want to kill him. But it was him or me."

He looked at her with stunned admiration. Then he noticed that she held her leg at a funny angle. And her lips were dangerously blue.

"Tarini, we have to get you out of here."

Austin eased her fully out of the ledge and held her to him, hoping the heat from his body would help bring her out of her violent shaking. He pulled back her chilly fingers from their grip on his jacket. He rubbed and blew at each precious digit to warm them. She talked tough, but she was clearly in shock—and had held herself together only with the last ounce of her strength.

If he took her anywhere—to any hospital or clinic or even a private doctor—he'd be signing her death warrant. The police would be alerted and authorities would be all over her in minutes. She'd be deported and he would have failed her.

Austin would have to pull her out of this on his own.

"Come on, Tarini, just walk to the clearing and

I'll carry you the rest of the way,'' he said, pulling her to her feet. "Just a little farther to the car..."

"Austin, something happened out there."

"Hey, Tarini, I know. And you acted like a pro."

"No, something else. I had this moment, when the baby moved. I realized what was important about my life and I knew what I had to do. Saving that baby's life gave me the strength to defend myself when I thought it was all over."

He eased her along the rough, rocky embankment. If he could just get her to the clearing, he could carry her the rest of the way to the car.

He had to keep her focused, but still, as she talked, he felt the strong connection with her. This was his baby she was talking about.

"What were you saying?"

"The baby moved," Tarini said, stumbling in front of him. He held his hands out to steady her. "The baby moved inside of me and then I realized that all my life I had been running away from my destiny, away from being pregnant, away from my womanliness, away from trusting any man. Away from trusting even you, Austin, even you. And when our baby moved inside of me, it changed me. It gave me all the strength I needed."

"Here, watch your feet. What in blazes are you talking about? Start from the top."

"I always wanted to deny my pregnancy," she said.

It was on the tip of his tongue to tell her that she had denied her pregnancy to him more than to herself, but he didn't. The bitterness within him was gone. Besides, he had a life to save, a job to do. And Austin Smith had never let anger get in the way of doing his job.

"I wanted to believe being pregnant, being a woman, made no difference in my life," she continued. "But it does. I am a woman who has a tiny life inside her."

"You're safe now," he said gently.

"I know. But I shouldn't have been in that position. I shouldn't have put myself in that position."

He would have explained each and every action that she had taken which had put her in danger, but he stopped himself. In fact, she was in that position because he had locked her up. And Tarini with a lock on her was an escape waiting to happen.

In the last hours, he had learned a lot about her—understood her even more than when he entered her in the most intimate way. He knew her now. Never lock her up because it was the surest way to make her run.

He picked her up and carried her the rest of the way to Bob's car, gently placing her in the front seat. In the trunk, he found a nubby wool blanket, and wrapped it around Tarini's lap. She was still shaking, but she was better. He slid into the driver's seat and turned the ignition. The first blast of air from the vents was cold, but quickly changed to tepid and then finally to warm. As the air in the car shook off its early spring chill, Tarini stopped shivering.

"Do you want to touch it?" she asked softly.

He looked at her—her face, illuminated only by the lights on the dash, gave away nothing.

"Touch what?" he asked cautiously.

"Your baby."

He gulped.

A theoretical baby was one thing—a daydream of football lessons he'd give in five years or of graduations he'd attend two decades from now, a battle with Tarini for honor and duty and doing the right thing. A theoretical baby was his name, his genetic mark, his family's heritage being passed on for another generation.

But a real baby—that was a another story. So near, so close, so incredible.

He realized he had been like Tarini—regarding this pregnancy as not making any fundamental changes in his life-style. Now, thinking of his hand on her stomach, he knew this baby would change everything about him.

He didn't know what to say.

She said it for him, taking his hand in her cold, trembling one. She lifted her T-shirt to let him touch the soft flesh beneath. Her stomach was hard, barely curved, and Austin wondered if Tarini hadn't just attributed a mystical experience to some simple indigestion.

They sat in silence for several moments. And then he thought he felt a movement in the flesh beneath his touch.

"Is that it?" he asked, openmouthed with wonder. "Is that our baby?"

"Yes. That's our baby."

He wanted to stay there, but he knew she was still in shock and he had to get her someplace warmer than Bob's car. Besides, eventually the authorities were going to head in their direction.

He took his hand back reluctantly and put the car in reverse.

"If it's a boy, we'll name him Vladimir," he said as he eased the car back onto the dirt road.

He knew that was the one thing—perhaps the only thing—they could agree on.

Chapter Twelve

They drove on side streets and back roads, and listened grimly to the updated news reports, which were uniformly depressing. She was a fugitive. If caught, she was going back to Byleukrainia. The dead liaison officer was some kind of war hero, according to the Byleukrainian government, and his death must be avenged.

But there was worse news. Byleukrainia had confirmed that Vlad was being held in prison. His crime? Being a Romanov, enemy of the people, although there were trumped-up charges of corruption and fraud so outrageous that no one but a true believer in the military government would credit them.

Unconfirmed reports asserted that Vlad's trial was being held at this very moment. There was no doubt as to the outcome. Rioting, killing, fires and looting had broken out in the Byleukrainian capital as Vlad's supporters erupted in fury and frustration.

Austin worried for his friend. But he was even more concerned with events nearer to home.

"Was it your mother or your sister who told Karinolov where we were?"

Tarini bristled. "Neither," she said crisply. "My mother would never speak to Karinolov and doesn't know where your parents live. She'd also have sense enough not to tell Tanya where I was headed."

"Then how did Karinolov know?"

"Bob."

"No way. He didn't even want to know where we were going. Remember? He specifically told me not to tell him so that he couldn't be forced by Karinolov to disclose our location. Bob's completely trustworthy."

"Maybe it was your father," Tarini ventured. "It's not unheard of for a diplomat to work as a spy. Even for a country that's not his own. Maybe he did it for money—after all, you have a pretty nice farm there considering he worked for the diplomatic corps all his life."

"Don't you dare accuse my father!" Austin said with indignation.

But, in the back of his mind, he wondered. His father had no allegiance to the Byleukrainian people, and if he thought Karinolov was the father of her child, he would have no interest in protecting Tarini, either.

"I still don't trust your sister. Tanya is under Karinolov's spell," he said at last.

"I don't trust her, either, but I know she wouldn't do anything to harm me."

"Let's agree to disagree on who's helping Karinolov," Austin said shortly, hoping she was wrong about the retired ambassador. "All I know is that Karinolov knew we were at my parents' house."

"Does he know where we are now?"

"No, because it's just you and me now, Tarini," Austin said, checking the rearview mirror. The two-lane highway was deserted and they hadn't seen another car for miles. "We won't go back to my parents'. You won't call your family. I won't call mine. We won't make contact with anyone. We both need a few hours of relative safety."

He found a roadhouse surrounded by six dilapidated cabins. He told the owner he was up for fishing and bought the smallest pair of jeans and a three-pack of men's undershirts from behind the counter of the attached fishing-and-hunting supply store.

The cabin wasn't the Ritz Carlton, but it was perfect for his purposes. The space was small, cozy, clean and it appeared that none of the other six cabins were occupied.

He carried her to the bed, stripping off her stained clothes, ignoring the urgent tangle of physical wants as he drew the plaid wool blanket around her neck.

She watched passively as he threw logs into the wood-burning stove and lit it with crumpled newspapers. He held her bloody T-shirt in his hands, thought of how close she had come to dying and threw it into the flames.

A crackle, a hiss, and he closed the stove.

While she dozed, he made two cups of decaf instant on the kitchenette hot plate. Then he drew a bath, waiting impatiently for the hot water to run. He tested it with his fingers, adjusted the temperature and came back into the bedroom. He thought she might be asleep and he would have simply sat on the cushioned wicker armchair beside the bed, but she whimpered.

In pain, in fear, he didn't know. But he did know that he had to help.

He picked her up and carried her to the bath. She didn't protest as he tugged off her bra and panties. Her ankle was swollen blue and he wondered how she had managed to get as far as she had—eight miles in two hours, it made him admire her all the more.

As he rubbed some antiseptic on a cut high on her forehead, she winced but didn't cry out. The blood on her knees and elbows looked horrible, but when she had soaked in the tub for a few minutes, the flesh revealed only minor scratches. All in all,

she had come out of the ordeal surprisingly un-
scathed.

And he was grateful.

"Nothing bad happened to the baby?" he asked.

She shook her head and looked away from him.

He knelt at the tub's edge and used the washcloth
to sluice warm water on her shoulders and back. He
pushed aside a few damp tendrils that covered her
eyes. "Feel better?" he asked.

"It will stay with me a long time, won't it?"

"Yeah," he said, knowing exactly what she
meant. Killing a man. "It will stay with you the
rest of your life. You'll always remember you did
it. But it won't feel this bad forever."

"Have you ever killed?"

"Yes. Once. I had to, just like you did. It was
him or me. He gave me no choice about that. And
that's the only way I ever think an honorable man
should ever kill. When he's faced with an enemy
that will only play for keeps."

"I hope I don't ever have to do it again."

"It's my job to make sure you're never in that
position again," he said softly.

Ordinarily he would have expected a lecture on
his politically incorrect views. Instead, she looked
up at him, eyes glittering with tears that she wiped
away before they could fall.

He would rather have had the lecture, because he
didn't like to see her broken up this way. He wished

he knew how to care for the emotional Tarini as well as he knew how to practice karate, fire a pistol or talk through a hostage situation.

"Are you really going to boss me around for the rest of my life?"

He chuckled. This wasn't the time for heavy emotions—this was the time to pull her out of this mess. "Tarini, I'm going to make your life hell," he said with mock severity.

"Why can't you just disappear, like all those—what do you call them?—deadbeat dads?"

"No, Tarini, I'm not that kind of man. You and this baby are stuck with me. I'll be very generous about alternating holidays."

"Alternating holidays?"

"Hell, I'll invite you over every Christmas, New Year's and Thanksgiving that I get with little Vladimir. I won't make you eat in the kitchen."

He wanted to tell her that it could be different. They could do it together. He could marry her. She could be his. They could have a family.

They could get a house in the suburbs. With enough land for a sandbox and a swing set and white picket fence to make sure the little tyke didn't run after a ball into the traffic.

Maybe even think about another baby.

Of course, she'd have to change her ways, get rid of that damnable independent streak, start thinking like a wife and mother.

Building a family sounded a lot better than arranging joint custody for the next twenty years.

And she had to know one thing—if he lived, he wasn't going to settle for less than full participation in raising this child.

They could marry...

Funny that Austin Smith, determined bachelor, would be thinking about weddings and home-cooked meals and buying a house in the suburbs.

A baby on the way did that to a man.

Besides, he loved her. And he was pretty sure that she'd kick up her heels like crazy, but she had a soft spot for him.

Then he remembered. She was a fugitive. His best friend was in a foreign prison.

He couldn't make any promises and he couldn't ask any of her when he didn't know for sure that they'd wake up tomorrow morning.

Or the next morning after that.

It was very possible they didn't have a future at all.

He could care for her tonight. He thought about the menu from the pizza-delivery shop that he had tucked into his coat pocket when he'd checked in. He should order her some dinner, something nutritious because she was eating for two, and then he should insist that she get some sleep.

Her doelike eyes blinked once, twice and again.

He smiled. She was tired, but being Tarini, wouldn't admit it.

He'd put her to bed and spend the rest of the evening planning their showdown with Karinolov. He wondered if he could at last persuade her to stay somewhere. Maybe he could rent a downtown hotel room and put Bob on detail to watch her. Or would it would be safer to have her in hand?

"Austin?" she said, interrupting his thoughts.

"What is it?"

She stood in the bath, water sluicing down her curves. He stared openmouthed. Her body was as taut and as exciting as ever. If anything, the only change pregnancy had wrought was to add greater fullness to her breasts.

His hardness was immediate and forceful. He didn't move, fearful he would lose control of himself.

"I'm finished with my bath," she said, her voice both wistful and inviting. "Why don't you get a towel?"

IN THE SHADOWS of the apartment building's staircase, Karinolov pulled away from Tanya, sighing. He made his appraisal as she looked up at him with large, chocolate-brown eyes.

She was pretty, in a fresh and innocent sort of way. Her kisses were like cotton candy—chastely sweet, unsatisfying but oddly addictive. He ran a coarse thumb over the flesh of her lower lip.

"Are you sure you can do this?" he asked.

"Will it save my sister?"

"Yes. It is the only way."

"She doesn't like you."

"I know," Karinolov said mildly. "And when you see her, she will say terrible things about me. But you can see the true me."

He took her hand and pressed it to his heart.

"Tanya, my darling. May I call you darling?" He paused, but didn't wait for the answer, which he knew would be yes. "Darling, you must go now. There is no time to waste."

"Let me just go upstairs and tell Mama."

"No," he said, restraining himself from being too forceful. "Go now. She will only try to persuade you to stay. You will argue and it will be upsetting for you both. It is late. Tarini needs you. Go now. Do you know exactly what to say and do?"

Tanya nodded. Karinolov marveled at her loyalty coupled with docile obedience to his will. Maybe it was because she was young and in love. He decided impulsively that he liked these traits in a woman, though he found those same characteristics repugnant in a man.

He escorted her to the waiting car.

As she settled into the driver's seat, he leaned

through the window and clasped her seat belt together with the tenderness of a lover.

He wished her luck and she drove off into the night. An aide stepped off the curb and came to his side.

"Have one of the men clip the apartment's telephone wires, just in case. And have your officers follow the two women back to the mission," Karinolov said, staring until the car disappeared around the corner. "From a good distance, because Tarini's smart enough she'll watch for someone tailing her."

"Yes, sir."

"And kill them both if they deviate from the route."

"Yes, sir."

And then Karinolov's face broke into an uncharacteristically revealing sneer.

His next task would give him great pleasure.

"I'll go upstairs and get Mama," he said.

Chapter Thirteen

Without taking his eyes from her face, he pulled a white terry towel from the rack on the wall and held it out to her. It took every bit of his self-control not to touch her, not to blot the droplets from every inch of her flesh.

Or to reignite a flame that he had so determinedly put out that terrible day in January when he realized she didn't want to see him anymore.

He willed himself not to stare at her precious curves.

She looked at the towel and then at him with an ambiguous innocence.

He pulled a sharp breath and stilled his response to her unspoken invitation.

"No, Tarini, please, I can't," he said, though he could. She had no idea how much he could.

And the old Austin, the one who kept his relationships with women simple, would have picked her up, wrapped her legs around his waist and steadied her on the vanity. And taken her. Swiftly, urgently, satisfying his own urgent needs while expertly bringing her to a shattering climax.

But making love to Tarini wasn't just about physical gratification anymore.

"Austin, please."

"I don't want to take advantage of you," he said, the truth sounding pitifully lame.

He should take her. Right here. As she asked him. He was ready, the force of his hardness quick and demanding. She was ready, he thought, giving himself permission to look at her. If the tremble of her upper thighs and her erect nipples were any indication, she wanted him every bit as much as he wanted her.

She took the towel and held it up against her modestly. As she did, her breasts strained up over the terry cloth in round globes.

He groaned.

She was as tormenting with a scanty towel held against her as she was naked.

"I want to, I really want to," he explained, hanging on to his self-control with only the barest thread of will. "I want you, Tarini, but I can't take advantage of you. You'll regret this."

"Why?"

"You're very vulnerable right now. You're in shock. You're not completely recovered."

"You always said I was a survivor."

"I never meant that as an insult or as an excuse for me."

"I could survive spending a few hours in bed with you," she said with a suggestive smile. "The question is—could you survive it?"

He felt uncomfortable with her repartee, although it was no different than the kind of sex talk they had used in December.

He had thought then that it was a sign of how much she was like him—how sophisticated and knowing, how experienced and epicurean in her tastes. He had never asked her about past lovers, but the way she had talked and teased about sex when they had come together in December, he had assumed there were men. At least a few.

She, like himself, was simply discreet about the past, he had assumed.

Now he knew, to the core of his being, that the playful sex talk had been an act, a role she had taken on so that he would regard her as an equal in bed.

But she hadn't been his equal.

She had been an innocent.

And he had been an unwitting predator. He had introduced her to lovemaking techniques that would put a blush on the most jaded call girl, and Tarini, not yet schooled in her own or in his needs, hadn't known enough to hold anything back.

She had learned from him the arts of pleasure so

quickly and eagerly that he had not noticed her hesitations. He'd thought that he had met his match.

And he had, but not in the way he'd imagined.

He winced at the sex talk now, knowing she was reaching out to him in the only way she thought he would respond to. *She must think I'm some kind of brute animal,* he thought.

"I can't do it, Tarini."

"Austin, I want you."

"I don't want you to hate me later," he said, running out of excuses. "I don't believe a man should do that to a woman."

"I thought you didn't mind me hating you," Tarini countered slyly. "In fact, I thought you hated me just as much as you think I hate you."

Austin squirmed. "I do. I mean, I did. Actually, I don't hate you. I never really did. I just felt betrayed and jerked around, but now I know you didn't mean any of it to hurt me. You were simply protecting yourself in the only way you knew how, and that I was—"

"Just shut up and kiss me. You're terrible at talking about feelings."

"Tarini, if I kiss you once, I'll want to kiss you again. And again. I won't stop. And you know what I can do when I don't stop."

"Yes. I know."

She looked at him archly. She wanted to forget so much and she thought she would in his arms. He suddenly understood that he could give her a night of pleasure that would heal her shock and terror of the day's events.

"Please, Austin," she pleaded softly.

It was the sudden stripping away of any coquettishness that drove home to him how much she needed him.

She reached out and placed her palm over the hardness that strained against his jeans. He grabbed her hand, intending to push it away.

But he couldn't.

The most beautiful woman he had ever known was pulling out all the stops, and at some point his self-control was shot.

Still, she couldn't be mercenary about this seduction—it wasn't in her nature. He noticed her haunted eyes searching his face. She wanted some reassurance.

Austin guessed it was because he had said nothing, absolutely nothing, about love. If he said the words "I love you" now, with no sanctuary to offer her, he'd be damning his honor. And Austin could never do that. Not if he couldn't protect her from Karinolov.

"Tarini, if I kiss you, I'll want to do more," he warned her one last time.

She dropped her towel. He groaned. She knew how to destroy his self-control.

"Did I say anything about less?" she asked.

HE CARRIED HER to the bedroom, which was lit by the glow emanating from the window of the stove. She slid under the worn but clean sheets. But as she pulled the wool blanket over her shoulders, she saw that Austin wasn't moving. He leaned against the wall watching her with knowing eyes.

She needed him. She had gone through so much in the last two days that she needed his strong embrace, his bruising kisses—oh, admit it, she admonished herself, she needed the release he gave her. The glorious feeling of teetering on the edge then careening down the roller coaster of sensation, held only by his safe, strong arms.

It was so honorable that he couldn't take advantage of a woman he regarded as having betrayed him in every possible way. He must sense her vulnerability, and ordinarily, she would admire his forbearance.

Funny how just the day before, just hours before, he had despised her, maybe deep down he still did. But he wouldn't harm her, and had come back for her—and had found her.

Now he was the only man who stood between her and death. He had faced guns, explosives, and would face down the law if caught harboring a fugitive. He had made her a promise on the New York sidewalk, that he would lay down his life for her. And he meant it.

And now he was scared to touch her.

But she wanted their lovemaking, if only to fool herself for a few hours that things were the way they had once been. She was seducing him and from the way his jeans strained against his body, she was doing pretty good.

She threw off the blanket and sheets. Kneeling on the bed, she put a pout on her face and posed seductively.

"Austin, you're very talented," she purred. "But you can't make love to me from all the way over there."

He narrowed his eyes.

She challenged him with a purposefully sultry look.

"Tarini, this isn't you."

Defeated, she felt the sting of salty tears in her eyes. "Austin, please, I beg you to remember what we shared," she said. "I don't know if I meant anything to you then, and I don't want you to make up any sentiments you don't really feel. But remember, we were good together. I need you, Austin, I need you to make love to me. I've been on the run, I've killed a man, I'm scared to death and I need you."

There. She had broken down and said it all. She closed her eyes and hoped the earth would open up and swallow her whole. She had debased and humiliated herself, and as she closed her eyes to the tears, she knew she hadn't even persuaded him.

And then she heard a button rolling across the floor, and her eyes flew up to him.

He yanked at the buttons of his denim shirt—but didn't pop any more of them—as he approached the bed. Feeling the glory of ardor, Tarini finished the job for him. Her hands lingered on the lattice of hard muscle underneath. Goose bumps rose on his flesh and then subsided as he released a low whistle of pleasure.

Her hand caught and recoiled from the barrel of the gun sticking out of the waistband of his jeans. He pulled it out and put it on the nightstand.

Gulping back the urge to drag him into bed—the slow undressing be damned—she unbuttoned his jeans.

As she reached, he grabbed her wrist. She looked up sharply. And noticed him looking at the ring on her hand.

Five carats' worth of being another man's woman.

"We never made love," she explained. "And Vladimir knew from the start that I was never really his."

"I feel funny."

"Do you want me to take it off?"

"No, I guess not," Austin said. "He is a brother to both of us, isn't he?"

Tarini nodded.

He unbuttoned his jeans. Then he put his wallet

beside the gun. Pulling his handcuffs out of his back pocket, he flung them down on the nightstand. He finished pulling off his jeans and then he stood before her, hard and strong. She leaned back against the pillows, watching him, feeling a mixture of pride and awe.

He was hers for pleasure—if only for the night.

"Come here," she said huskily. "I can't wait much longer." She knew it would be good.

He slid on top of her, holding his weight on his elbows so that he didn't crush her. His flesh against hers satisfied a longing she hadn't known was so deep, and ignited a fire she hadn't expected to burn so hot. She wanted him inside her, wanted to take every inch of him, but she knew from experience he liked to take his time, to draw things out in lingering and exquisite torment.

"I won't hurt you, will I?" he asked abruptly.

"I'm just pregnant, not an invalid."

"There's nothing 'just' about it. Don't let me do anything that will harm the baby."

She brought him close to her face, but as she led him, he took over. He kissed her, exploring every inch of her mouth with his tongue, sucking her lower lip, and then relinquishing her just as she could bear no more of his sweetness.

She rubbed her hips against him, and still he hung back, holding his manhood inches from her pleasure, his hard thighs entwined with hers but contracted just shy of union.

The touch excited but did not satisfy.

"You're not going to hurt me," she urged.

"You're sure?"

She nodded.

And it was as if he were an animal that had been released from its restraints. He took her flesh as his, and though he caressed the core of her womanhood with his palm to bring her to readiness, she stopped him. He had introduced her to many variations of ecstasy in their brief affair, but she wanted only one thing tonight.

She wanted him on top of her, inside of her, between her legs. Taking her as his woman.

"Now, Austin," she urged again.

She didn't have to say more, he didn't ask what she wanted. He knew. They were both fluent in their own language of lovemaking. He joined his body with hers with a deep, powerful thrust. She wrapped her strong, sleek legs around him.

And then he held nothing back.

They came together, in shuddering moans. He buried his head in the base of her neck. She thought she heard him call her name. She wanted him to, wanted to hear him want her and no other woman. She wanted to believe that she had been forgiven for her deceptions and that they had a chance together.

She felt the final concentric spasms of her orgasm. And then came the exhaustion she had denied so long. The quiet was broken by a log dropping on the stove's grill.

"Tarini, I'm sorry I doubted you," Austin said, rolling off her and pulling her into a spoonwise embrace. "You *were* a virgin, weren't you?"

"Yes," she admitted. "There's never been another man."

"Why didn't you tell me at the time?"

"I didn't want you to know because I thought it would scare you."

"It would have made all the difference in the world. I couldn't have made love to you."

"And now?" she asked.

"Now I wonder how badly I've taken advantage of you. In December. Tonight. Here."

Tarini felt a cold stillness though he lay snug against her back, his arms cradling her.

"Taken advantage of me?" she asked hollowly.

"Yes."

Tarini, you are a fool, she thought. His words didn't sound like love, didn't mention a future, didn't hold out any hope. He wasn't making any promises and he wasn't asking her for any. That was Austin—how he had been and how he was now.

She had liked that quality in him before, had seen it as hardheaded realism in an uncertain world. After all, where would anybody be in a year, in two, in a decade? Besides, Austin for a husband was unthinkable. He was too independent.

And besides, what American could fathom the odd customs and traditions of Byleukrainian culture? Tarini had enough trouble figuring out all things American and she didn't doubt that Austin would have trouble understanding anything about Byleukrainia that hadn't been taught to him by Vlad. Even with the years of practice at tolerance and appreciation of others that diplomatic life gives, Austin could be pretty pigheaded about learning new things.

Still, something had happened to her when the gun went off on that riverbed. When she had killed, when she had come this close to death. When she had a baby to protect and suddenly felt that primal need to find a man's strength to shield her for the coming months.

Not just any man would do. Only the father of her baby. Only her husband—because that's what a father to her baby must be.

That's how traditional my thinking goes in an emergency, Tarini thought wryly. So much for modern womanhood. She felt safety only in his arms.

"You haven't taken advantage of me," she said stiffly. "You said it yourself. I'm a survivor. Besides, I'm the one who did the asking. Tomorrow we'll forget this.''

''Is that how you want it?''

No! Her mind screamed.

But she was proud. She had gone down on her knees to bring him to her bed, she wasn't going to beg for a ring or a relationship or even for him to buy her a cup of coffee in the morning.

''Fine with me,'' she said casually.

He stared at her but she looked away.

So they weren't headed for the altar. They were headed for some lawyer's office, where they'd work out weekends and holidays and who would pick their child's summer camp.

It looked like a fate nearly as terrible as being deported.

''Tarini?'' Austin asked softly. ''Does it have to be this way?''

She bit back a sharp retort which would have reminded him that ''this way'' was his choice, not hers. Instead, she rolled over with her back to him and murmured that she was too sleepy to think straight.

The truth was, her thinking was as straight as it had ever been. She had made love to him and it had been physically pleasurable. She should leave it at that.

At last, she felt Austin's breath still and she knew that the harrowing day had finally caught up with him, even as her nervous energy kept her thoughts racing. She had to know before he fell into sleep.

"What are we going to do next?" she asked quietly, kicking his leg gently to awaken him.

He moaned and stirred. "I have to persuade Karinolov to leave you and the baby alone," he groaned.

"How will you do that?"

"Either I'll be on my knees or I'll be a gun against his forehead. I haven't really formulated a plan. In any event, you're not going. You're taking our child into hiding. I'm taking you into the city. Bob will watch you. Understand?"

"No way."

"He's the only man I trust completely, Tarini. He'll protect you."

"You'd be putting his family in danger if I stayed at their apartment."

"Bob will take you someplace safe."

"And what about Vlad?"

Silence. And then the heavy words that cut into her heart.

"I think we've lost whatever chance we had to rescue him—at least for the moment. The baby has to come first. I'm sure Vlad would understand."

But Tarini knew that Austin was the one who didn't understand. Tarini knew that, against all the evidence, Austin regarded the kidnapping as his own fault, as his failing of a friend. She also knew that relinquishing the hope of finding Vlad destroyed what was most vital about his manhood.

"As soon as Karinolov knows I'm not carrying a Romanov baby, he'll back off," Tarini said confidently.

"No, not at all," Austin replied. "You were engaged to Vlad, however briefly. No matter where you are, no matter how we raise our child, the rumors will always be there."

"So what will we do?"

"I may have to send you into hiding."

Tarini suppressed a retort at the assumption that he had to do something about her at all. "Like the federal witness-protection system?" She asked instead. "Forget it. Because I won't leave my family behind."

"Your mother would understand the stakes. And your sister is a traitor."

"My sister is a foolish young girl!"

"Let's not start that again."

The air crackled with silent tension. A standoff.

"Tarini?" Austin asked. "You aren't hatching some kind of plan, are you? Because I'd like to get some sleep before I take on Karinolov, and I can only do it if I know that you're not going to run off on one of your disastrous escapades."

Tarini glared at his pillow.

"And don't swear under your breath at me in your native language," he warned. He didn't open his eyes. "You forget, I can understand everything you're saying. I don't appreciate being referred to as the underbelly of a cow."

"Then I'll say it in English—you're a controlling, domineering, pigheaded…"

Click.

Tarini stared at her wrist in horror.

He had cuffed her to the headboard in one swift motion and then had rolled over with a pillow over his head as if he was going right back to sleep.

He really was a—

"Don't say it," Austin warned.

Chapter Fourteen

"You just cuffed me!"

"Yeah, I did," Austin groaned from under the pillow.

"You can't do this to me!"

Though Austin kept his head under the pillow, his words came through loud and clear.

"I can and I did."

"It's barbaric."

"And absolutely necessary if I'm going to sleep."

"You just made love to me and now you're making me a prisoner!"

He pulled his head out from under the pillow and looked at her with weary eyes.

"Tarini, maybe I was wrong to make love to you. But while you can ask for my apology, you can't make me feel guilty enough to take those cuffs off."

"But..."

"Maybe I took advantage of you, but there are many men who would have done the same in my shoes. You gave me every signal in the world that you wanted to make love as much as I did. I felt good. And, you did, too."

"I did feel good! But..." Her words faltered, but her outrage did not. "But I didn't ask to be put in cuffs afterward! You're acting like a territorial animal. You make love to me and then want to own me."

"This has nothing to do with ownership," He said bluntly. "Tarini, I'm warning you. I'll do anything to get a good night's sleep. If handcuffs aren't enough, I've got a handkerchief in my jeans pocket to tie around your mouth and I've got a length of rope in the trunk of Bob's car that'll go nicely around your—"

She shivered. "I get the picture," she interrupted regally. "Go to sleep, macho man."

"I'm planning on it, little lady," he said blithely.

With a frustrated growl, he turned over and jammed the pillow back over his head.

Tarini yanked at the cuff. The headboard was solid. The cuffs were locked.

"You're not going anywhere tonight," Austin muttered from beneath his pillow. "So why don't you just go to sleep? I'm sure you could use some."

She rattled the cuffs a few times, to show she could make his night hell, regardless. But he didn't respond. And after a while she got tired of goading him.

She was trapped.

She stared at the man beside her.

"I don't think I can bring up this baby with you in the picture," she concluded aloud. "I think the idea of our doing anything so important as raising a child together is ludicrous."

"Give me the baby when it's born and you won't have to."

"I'm not giving up my own child!"

"Then you'll have to learn to do what I tell you to do," he said, pulling his head out from under the pillow. "Starting with this—you're not getting anywhere near Karinolov. I take care of Karinolov. You take care of the baby."

He lay down, clearly satisfied with how he had assigned their responsibilities. Within minutes he was asleep.

But as his breath grew quiet and rhythmic, Tarini brooded and fidgeted and swore at herself for having given an inch to this testosterone cowboy.

She stared at the ceiling, spidery with plaster-repair jobs made over the years.

Having a baby with this man was like signing herself into prison. A prison in which the warden had the two most potent deterrents to escape: her child and her own wantonness.

Even now, as he stretched in sleep and rolled

over onto his back, she wanted to caress the ladder of muscles running down his stomach, she wanted to stroke the golden curls at his groin, to take in her hand the rising manhood.

"Get a grip, Tarini," she whispered. "You're not going to be his serf."

She threw the sheet over his body and promised herself that she'd never, ever give in to temptation again.

Then she noticed Austin's jeans lying on the floor just five feet from the bed. Where he had dropped them in the striptease that had been her undoing.

Men never put away their clothes, she thought with annoyance that soon turned into a self-satisfied smile. Now that basic and universal biological fact was about to set her free.

"So I have to learn to do what you tell me, huh?" she whispered to Austin.

But he slept on, oblivious even as she slid the bed out from the wall the bare inches she needed to reach the jeans with her foot. She dragged the jeans toward her with her big toe grasping a belt loop.

Once she had them, she fished his key chain out of his pocket and unlocked the cuffs. Her wrists felt red and raw and her ankle throbbed angrily. She might be in the middle of nowhere, but she was free.

She looked at Austin, a slow smile coming to her lips. A smile that didn't reach her eyes.

"We could have been..." Her smile faltered, and she couldn't finish her sentence.

It wasn't any fun to taunt him while he slept. Or when she was walking out on him.

AFTER QUICKLY DRESSING in the clean clothes he had purchased for her, she hobbled toward the pay phone at the side of the roadhouse. She emptied her purse on the ground, pulled out enough change to buy an orange soda and a bag of chips from the vending machine—the rest she used for the call.

A chill went through her when no one answered the phone at her mother's apartment. At one o'clock in the morning? Where was her mother? Where was her sister? Was Tanya with Karinolov?

On a dreadful hunch, she placed a second call to the mission.

"Ah, Tarini, I've been waiting to hear from you," Karinolov's smooth-as-silk voice answered.

"Look, call off your men and stay away from my sister," Tarini said. "This isn't Vlad's baby."

"A nice try, but hardly convincing. And drearily expected."

"It's Austin's child."

There was a sharp breath and then silence.

She hadn't wanted to tell him that she carried Austin's child, aware of the deep personal hatred between the two men. Still, she had spoken the truth. And surely Karinolov would respond to the truth.

" 'A' for effort, Tarini. Still, I don't believe you. Austin doesn't strike me as the kind of man who would allow the woman who's carrying his child to get out of his grasp. You are the fiancée of a Romanov. You carry his child."

"Vladimir is sterile."

"Ha! Much more creative, but still, Tarini, that's impossible."

She explained everything and waited for him to digest the new information.

"Tarini, you are to come here immediately," he said shakily.

"I wouldn't get near you if—"

"I've got your mother."

"My mother!"

Tarini was shocked. Her sister she could understand being at the mission, but Mama? She clutched the telephone receiver more tightly, willing herself to stay cool and think clearly. "Prove it."

"I don't have to."

He hung up.

Tarini stared at the receiver and then, as the dial tone came on, she hung up. She looked at the cabin where Austin slept. She could go to him, tell him that Karinolov might have her mother. But he would charge into danger alone—something Tarini couldn't bear when her mother's life was at stake.

She trudged up to the road, trying to ignore the pain in her ankle. Headlights appeared over the distant hill. She put out her thumb and waited. A light blue Nissan pulled to a halt.

"It couldn't be," Tarini murmured.

But the passenger-side window slid open, revealing Tanya's pixieish face.

"Oh, Tarini, I'm so glad I found you!" she cried out. "I've been driving up and down these roads for hours. I had just about given up."

Tarini slid into the car and the sisters hugged each other. As she pulled back from Tanya's embrace, Tarini shoved away her suspicions at how Tanya had found her.

Tanya was no professional, she was an amateur. But an amateur in love with a dangerous man.

"Tanya," Tarini said, studying her sister carefully. "How did you find me?"

"I told you! I've been driving for hours. When I heard about the shooting, I drove up here," she exclaimed, reaching into the back seat to produce a torn, crumpled road map. "I've been down every one of these streets. Connecticut is the most confusing place I've ever been to."

"What about...Karinolov? Tanya, you must know that he's—"

"I know," Tanya interrupted. "He's evil, absolutely evil. I've found it out for myself. I was wrong. Totally wrong. Forgive me, Tarini."

"Oh, I do," Tarini said, drawing her sister into her embrace.

Tanya was the first to pull away.

"We have to get back to New York. Tarini, he has Mama! At the mission. We must save her."

As her sister burst into tears, Tarini felt a mixture of relief and despair. Relief that her sister had finally learned the truth about Karinolov, and despair at the confirmation that her mother was in danger. She comforted her sister and then realized that now was the time for action.

"I'll drive," she said. And, without complaint, Tanya slid into the passenger seat as Tarini limped around to the driver's-side door.

THE MOMENT Austin awakened, he felt the chill at his back and knew she was gone. He reached to flip on the lamp.

His arm wouldn't move.

The cold steel tightened every time he reflexively yanked at the headboard. She had cuffed him. He swore.

The phone rang. His eyes narrowed as he picked up. It was Karinolov. Somehow he wasn't surprised.

"Congratulations, Austin," Karinolov said.

Austin fought the urge to hang up. He twisted his body around so that he'd be more comfortable.

As comfortable as he could be in handcuffs.

"For what?"

"For becoming a father. I hadn't known about Vlad. If this bizarre story about measles is true, your child could have been raised as a Romanov."

"It's true. Believe it," Austin said grimly. "How'd you find out?"

"She called."

"Where is she?"

"She's on her way to New York," Karinolov said breezily. "She thinks she's saving your life and freeing you to work your mischief on behalf of that damnable Romanov. And I have her mother here. Tarini will do anything for the people she loves. Self-sacrificing heroine, wouldn't you say? Too bad she's not one of us. Of course, we need people who are a little more cold-blooded and a lot less...trouble."

Austin studied the cuff and then glanced over at the nightstand. Where were the damn keys? His sheet fell away and he realized he was naked. It had felt good when her body was near to him, skin to skin. But now nakedness only made worse the terrible sensation of being exposed.

"What do you want from me?" Austin demanded, tugging at the cuffs and drawing a red, angry welt on his wrist as they tightened even more.

Karinolov laughed maliciously. "Just the satisfaction of knowing I've hurt you in a way even more enduring than killing you."

"And how is that?"

"I'm taking your firstborn," Karinolov taunted. "And your woman. Oh, sure, you can try again—another child, another woman. For the renowned playboy Austin Smith, there are plenty of other women. And many other opportunities to have a child, though you've never been regarded as particularly domestic. But whatever you do, wherever you go, if you die tomorrow trying to save Vlad or if you live to a hundred and ten, you'll never have this child and this woman."

"Don't hurt her!" Austin pleaded. He scanned the room, looking for the keys. She couldn't have been so cruel as to take those, too.

"It doesn't matter, really, the part about the measles," Karinolov continued. "She was his fiancée, she wears the Romanov ring. The rumors about her child would be even more damning than the ones in that regrettable Anastasia case."

"She has nothing to do with any of this."

"Not so," Karinolov disagreed. "You know, when I thought she was carrying Vladimir's child, I was almost inclined to offer her a deal."

"A deal?"

"That I would marry her, shielding her from the extremists in my government who would want her dead, and I would raise Vlad's child as my own. I thought it would have been a particular irony to take the last Romanov and turn him into a Karinolov peasant. But now, I don't feel so inclined. An American whelp in her belly.'' He snorted in disgust. ''She's as good as dead. Maybe I'll take her sister as my own. She's not quite as desirable as Tarini, but she'll do.''

Austin reflexively jerked his fist, but was caught short by the cuffs. ''Don't do anything to Tanya!'' Austin shouted, wondering how the honor of his woman's family had become his own. ''Don't do anything to either of them. I'll come down. We'll fight this out. Man to man. You choose the terms.''

''I'm so pleased.'' Karinolov smirked. ''I've finally figured out that you're just the kind of misguidedly honorable man who would feel the pain of this loss more deeply than any other injury I could inflict. Such a pity I have to send Tarini back to the homeland.''

''Don't!''

Karinolov's laughter was sharp and without humor. ''When you beg for her life, it fills me with pleasure. I've got you, Austin, I've really got you now.''

Austin felt the tightness in his chest swell and then release as he came to a decision. He was a man of honor, respectful of the rule of law. But he was also a father.

The law had no punch. But that wouldn't stop Austin. He had made his choice between what was right and what was legal.

"I'm coming down," he said.

"I'll be waiting," Karinolov said cheerfully before hanging up.

Austin threw down the phone and then tugged at his cuffs. The metal jangled against the brass headboard. Think clearly, he cautioned himself. His eyes scanned the room and rested on his jeans. He'd find a way to get out.

TEN MINUTES LATER, he was standing at the door of Bob's car. Something bothered him, some feeling he couldn't shake. He had missed something, some intuition he had ignored.

He remembered the moments before his car had blown up in the Manhattan parking lot, the feeling of being watched.

He closed the driver's-side door and crouched beside the car, running his hand along the grillwork. Finding nothing, he checked the front of the car, opening the hood to caress every available surface area.

And then, underneath the passenger-side door, he found it. A tiny sensor, no bigger than a dime, attached to the inside of the hood with a piece of black electrical tape.

He yanked hard and dislodged it.

He would have missed it, but his father had shown him so many similar transmitters and sensors over the years.

Austin threw the sensor deep into the woods and tried not to think too much about the implications. He had to stay focused—

Find Tarini and beg, kill or be killed for her life.

Chapter Fifteen

"We're here," Tarini said, pulling into a parking space a block from the mission. Her grim-faced sister nodded and unbuckled her seat belt.

Chaos ruled the square in front of the U.N. mission's gates. Several hundred Byleukrainians carried posters and banners demanding an end to the military rule of their country. They screamed anti-military slogans. When television cameras approached, some who had relatives back home hid their faces, while others more brazenly told reporters of the horrors of the new regime. So many of them had relatives whose deaths were at the hands of the new military government.

Tarini kept her head down, averting her eyes and praying no one would recognize her or her sister. She didn't want to be delayed on her mission to find her mother. She led Tanya around to the alley.

She knocked twice, shivered and pulled Austin's

ripped, bloodstained quilted jacket around herself. She gave her sister's arm a reassuring squeeze.

"I'm sorry," Tanya said, her eyes downcast.

"It's all right."

"No, it's not…"

The door opened and the yeasty, oddly comforting smell of the kitchen drew the two women in. Karinolov stood alone in the shadows by the door to the dining room.

"Where's my mother?" Tarini demanded.

"I'm so glad you could come," he said with the ease of a dinner-party host.

Tarini let the heavy steel door fall shut behind her. Tanya slipped out from around her and stood near the table. Karinolov stepped forward and touched Tarini's cheek.

"Such smooth skin. Flawless, really. And your eyes, the color of emeralds. No wonder a Romanov would put his ring on your finger," Karinolov said and then his voice turned ugly. "Too bad you have soiled yourself with an American."

Tarini willed herself not to flinch, not to give him the satisfaction of seeing her fear.

From the alcove, she saw a shadow and then her mother appeared. A tall, proud woman—she had a bruise on her cheek and she flashed Karinolov a look of revulsion.

"Mama!" Tanya cried out, rushing to her mother's embrace.

"Such a touching scene," Karinolov muttered.

Tanya turned from her mother's arms to look at Karinolov, her eyes glittering with tears. "You never said you were really going to involve Mama!"

TARINI HAD WALKED into his trap. And there was no way out. She looked at the purse that he had taken from her as he'd slipped off her jacket in an act of seeming gentlemanliness. Her mother held her youngest daughter close, as Tanya sobbed uncontrollably.

Though Tanya had gotten her into this mess, Tarini's heart went out to her sister. Tanya had been betrayed by the man she idolized, whom she had loved from a distance for so long and from up close for a whirlwind few days.

But Tarini couldn't think about that now. She had to focus on saving her family.

The purse was too far away on the kitchen counter, the gun hopelessly crammed at the bottom of the bag. Besides, a brawny security guard lurked in the shadows near the butler's pantry. If she tried anything at all, she would be cut down.

And her mother and sister...? She didn't trust herself to be faster than the guard and Karinolov.

She kept her face impassive and stepped into the light of the kitchen. Struggling to keep her knees from buckling, she followed Karinolov through the regal dining room.

Empty now, stripped of its treasured tiger-maple furniture, wondrous paintings, and collection of crystal plates.

Empty Plexiglas cabinets and empty walls with solitary hooks made clear Karinolov had taken the best of the mission's Byleukrainian national treasures.

She didn't flinch as she was led to the foyer, but her stomach turned and her throat dried up. The crate. It was there, waiting for her.

She would be transported to whatever hell they planned for her in a space so tight, so cramped and black, that Tarini was sure she would go crazy. Even looking at it made her tethered nerves nearly snap.

She glanced back to her mother and sister who had been menaced into the dining room by a guard with an AK-47. Her sister's sobs had turned to hysterics as Tanya seemed to begin to understand that the betrayal at Karinolov's hands had implications far more devastating than the damage to her heart.

Tarini looked into her mother's eyes. To an outsider, her mother might appear to be unnaturally calm. But Tarini knew the fear and heartache—when Tarini was just a child and her mother pregnant with Tanya, they had fled the fighting in the capital of Byleukrainia. It had taken four long years to find safety in America.

Tanya didn't remember, but Tarini did.

And now in her mother's eyes, she saw that the responsibility for the family had passed from mother to eldest daughter.

Tarini only hoped she could bargain for safety for her family.

"Tarini, a pregnant woman must keep up her strength," Karinolov said soothingly, offering her a plate of traditional sweetmeats. "As you can see, your accommodations have no dining amenities and it's a long journey to the capital. Besides, the food back home is not going to be of this quality. You're not being returned to the palace, you know."

Tarini hadn't eaten since chugging an orange soda and munching a few chips at the roadhouse vending machine. But the sight of the delicacies made her sick.

She glared at him. But she knew there wasn't much she could do. Even kneeing him in the groin would probably cost her her life—she counted ten bodyguards who had taken up positions in the shadows of the staircase and the hallways leading away from the foyer.

Tarini wondered how they could spare this much security just for her—the crowds outside were getting more noisy and urgent. Someone had lobbed eggs at the stained-glass window over the front doorway, the gooey whites and yolks sliding down the outside of the panes.

Tarini wondered how Karinolov expected to get her out of here, and then remembered that the law required the police to offer safe passage to an ambassador traveling with a courier package.

She would be the courier package.

Not that they really posed any threat to Karinolov. A few hundred protesters didn't even know she existed. And to think she had never wanted her mother to know—to find out that she was pregnant. What a silly worry that seemed now, and as she glanced at her mother, she noted there was no censure in those eyes.

Her mother would have welcomed Austin into her home, even if he was an American. And she would have thrilled to hold a grandchild in her arms.

She held up her head defiantly. Might as well be like Vlad and go out with some dignity, she thought.

"So that's how you're going to be," he said coolly, passing the tray into the hands of a servant. "We could have been good together."

"No, we couldn't. I'm a human being. And you're not."

"You sound so incredibly bitter." Karinolov tilted his head back and stared at her. "I could kill you now, but my government is very adamant that you come back alive."

"I'll tell the world about your hideous crimes."

"No, you won't. You're going to die before you get to tell anyone else," Karinolov said, recovering his sangfroid. "It'll be our secret that you will take to...the Romanov grave."

"Am I going where Vlad is?" she asked, wondering if at least she'd have a chance to see him before she died.

"Yes, as a matter of fact, you are going back there—to him. The Romanov family will be reunited in their deaths."

"What about my mother and sister?"

"Ah, the Schaskylavitch women," Karinolov mused aloud. "Last of the line of a respected, noble family."

He sauntered over to Tanya, who cowered in her mother's embrace. He touched her cheek and ran his fingers through her tousled hair. Tanya lashed out and raked him with her nails, drawing a pinprick of blood and an angry line of welts.

Tarini admired her sister's courage. Karinolov touched the drop of blood, tasted it and shrugged.

Then he looked at Tarini.

"Because I once loved you when I was young and you were the spoiled child of a wealthy aristocrat," Karinolov said, "for you, Tarini, in memory of that childish love, I shall give you my word.

They will live. Always with the knowledge that they owe their lives to you. And to the mercy I bestow on your behalf."

"You loved my daughter?" Mrs. Schaskylavitch asked.

"Only from a distance," Karinolov said. "I was a young soldier posted in the capital. Not good enough to be invited to the Schaskylavitch home."

"We never judged people on the basis of their wealth," Mrs. Schaskylavitch protested.

"I would watch her as she played, and once..."

"Once you gave me candy and touched me on the cheek," Tarini cried out, the revolting memory bubbling to the surface of her consciousness, the makings of every nightmare. "You told me one day you would own me and my family, as well."

"And I was right."

"You'll never get away with this," Tarini said, trying to hold on to her composure.

Karinolov grunted. "You and Austin keep saying I won't get away with this or that." He shrugged. "But I have no worries. Justice is made by the conquerors. When you and Vlad are punished for your crimes against the people—"

"Vlad is poised to take back the country," Tarini said quietly. "There is rioting in the streets of the capital."

"Vlad is a wimp and a child. He is also, my dear,

in prison. And if he got out, he would head straight
for the cushy safety of America.''

"No, he wouldn't. He would lead his country in
a revolt."

"He would protect himself."

"You're crazy and you're evil."

"I might be crazy and I might be evil," Karinolov admitted, "but I'm the one in charge. Now
get in the box."

Tarini began to shake—not a ladylike tremble but
wiggly, legs-turn-to-jelly shakes.

She couldn't do it. But there wasn't any other
choice.

She could make a break for it, but the guards
around the foyer made it clear what her fate would
be—instant death. For her and her baby.

She could try to hurt Karinolov. But she couldn't
put her sister and mother in danger.

How she had been wrong, about so many things!
She needed Austin so badly now, she knew she
loved him, and she had never told him. Always
waiting for him to say something—she should have
told him she loved him and if he didn't return her
feelings, so what? At least her heart would be truth-
ful.

As for surrendering herself to his rule? Maybe it
hadn't been quite so black-and-white. Maybe both
of them had been scared to bend even a little bit,
for fear of losing all that they had.

Her only comfort was that, with handcuffs tying him to a bed in a Connecticut fishing cabin, Austin wasn't in danger.

"He's not coming," Karinolov said, seemingly reading her thoughts. "You wouldn't think that we'd lay a trap for you and not for him?"

"Where is he?" Tarini begged.

"Taken care of. After all, you led us to him."

She felt her stomach turn. "How…?"

He shook his head. "My secret, Tarini."

"Oh, Austin, all I've ever brought you is trouble," she moaned, thinking of him lying naked, defenseless, cuffed to a bed. She was sure he woke when they'd come in on him, and if he had thought about her in his final moments, he would have known that she had brought him nothing…nothing but trouble.

She angrily swiped away the tears that dampened her cheeks.

"Your sentiments of love are so damn touching," Karinolov growled, all pretense of civility erased. "Just get in the box."

A bodyguard entered the foyer.

"Ambassador, a few of the protesters have broken through the gate and are now on the grounds."

Tarini brightened. Maybe…?

"Shoot them," Karinolov barked.

"You can't do that!" Tarini exclaimed.

"We can," Karinolov said tersely. "Diplomatic

immunity is such a versatile thing. Other countries have done precisely the same in similar circumstances. And do you know what the police will do?''

''They'll arrest you.''

''They'll do absolutely nothing,'' Karinolov corrected triumphantly. ''Oh, sure, there might be a protest. A few denunciations from the United States government. But you'll be dead by then. Now, get in the crate. We could have had something special—however briefly—but you'd rather go to your death quickly.''

She hesitated. After all, Austin was dead. She had loved him and had never had the chance to let him know.

We're survivors, she heard his words. *That's what I admire about you. A survivor hangs on until the very end.*

And if she loved him, if she truly loved him, she would use her last breath, her last moment of life, to save their child and to reach Vlad. The chances were slim, the possibility of any success small—but she had to try.

She took a deep, final breath of freedom. She glanced at her mother, saw the love, the memory of which would have to sustain her. Fighting her terror, she crouched into the box. Karinolov tightened the leather restraints.

''Just so that you know that I'm not without the

quality of mercy," Karinolov said at her ear, as he pulled a hypodermic needle from inside his jacket pocket. "I'm giving you a little something."

She shook her head fiercely. No drugs! She fought against Karinolov's touch, thinking of her baby, frantic that whatever was in that needle could harm him. But what would it matter now that her death was a certainty?

A quick jab of a needle in her forearm, a full sensation in her muscles. And then Karinolov's loathsome kiss on her cheek.

Tarini struggled against the sudden heaviness of her limbs. She wanted to stay alert. She heard her mother's protest, cut short by an order barked by Karinolov.

She heard the bodyguards hammer the last nails of the lid, knew they were affixing the seals of the official diplomatic courier of the Byleukrainian mission. Tarini let her tears come in the darkness of her tiny prison. She wouldn't give them the satisfaction of her sobs.

She thought of Austin, of the brief pleasures she'd shared with him. After all, so many people are given no happiness. At least she'd had happiness in his arms.

And then the drug Karinolov had given her kicked in. She felt the last of her fight go out of her. She was floating, her muscles limp, her eyes drooping shut.

A final image: she thought of the guest bedroom in the Smiths' Connecticut farmhouse. She was lying on the chintz bed, a beautiful baby boy kicking in her arms, Austin at their side, looking on with joy, with pride, with love.

All gone.

It could have been that way.

She knew that fantasy would have to last her forever.

Chapter Sixteen

"Couldn't you at least have washed the car before you brought it back?"

Bob shoved his hand up on the dashboard and reflexively kicked his feet in front of him in a useless attempt to control the speeding vehicle.

But Austin was in the driver's seat. That meant two-wheel turns and a decided lack of interest in using the brakes. Down Park Avenue and spinning around the corner of Madison Avenue and East Fifty-third Street as if on a dime.

"Just be grateful I put a full tank of gas in this thing," Austin said tightly.

Austin's concentration was focused entirely on the traffic, and the odds of reaching the mission in time. It had taken him nearly a half hour to find the keys to the cuffs, and his wrists still hurt.

Austin decided if he found Tarini in time, he'd use something besides cuffs to hang on to her.

That woman was trouble!

Bob checked in on the mike attached to his uniform's jacket.

"Uh, Austin, I got some bad news," he said. "Looks like the mission is surrounded. Maybe we better swing into Paley Park and ditch the car."

"Two blocks! It's just two more blocks!" Austin screamed. "We're almost there!"

"That's what I wanted to talk to you about, buddy."

"Oh, God." Austin whistled as he brought the car to a screeching halt.

The block around the mission was in chaos. The shots fired from inside had injured a young woman on the grounds and had provoked blood rage in the crowd. The ornate iron gates had been toppled and the flag of the military regime burned on the courtyard. Hundreds of protesters screamed, cried, sang the Royalist national anthem until they were hoarse. They pounded on the leaded-glass door of the mission until, with a heaving cry, it gave way.

Then, with police desperately trying to restore order, the mob stormed the marble-floored foyer and spilled into the ballrooms and studies and offices of the diplomatic mission.

The angry mob paused only for moment of awe for the meager artifacts that Karinolov had not stripped from the ballroom. One woman ripped apart the poster from the days of Communist rule.

Police had cordoned off the block with bright

yellow sawhorses, but news had leaked of the riot
and the people could not be held back.

Immigrants angered by events in their homeland
saw the taking of the mission as an opportunity to
assert their love for the Byleukrainia of long ago
and they swarmed over the sawhorses and the stra-
tegically parked squad cars.

Local news crews spilled from vans with station
affiliates emblazoned on their sides. A matched set
of ambulances and fire trucks parked up on the sidewalk of East Fifty-fourth Street.

A policeman paced with a bullhorn, powerlessly
urging the crowd to disperse. But there was no
calm.

In uniform, Bob was given no trouble by the police as he escorted Austin onto the mission grounds.
While the police might be gaining tentative control
of the perimeter, the mission itself belonged to the
people.

Austin shoved Bob ahead of him through the
crowd of protesters and up the back stairs that no
one had discovered yet.

The penthouse-floor personal diplomatic apartment was undisturbed, though the noise from below
was deafening. The crowd would soon find the
channel of narrow stairs that led to the private
chambers.

Austin had to work fast. He didn't have a moment to waste. He ripped open the desk drawers and flipped through files and documents.

"What are you looking for?" Bob asked as Austin rifled through papers on the desk.

"Anything that tells me where the hell they've taken Tarini," Austin replied. "She's not here. They've gotten ahead of us—otherwise they would have mowed down every man, woman and child that's downstairs now."

"Are you in love with her?"

Austin stared at Bob. "Yes," he answered carefully.

Bob looked down at the ground.

"Where did they take Tarini?" Austin asked.

The two friends looked at each other.

"We can't stop them," Bob moaned. "That monster is still the ambassador. We can't do anything."

The fax blurted a reply. A couple of high-pitched squawks and then a chattering that went on and on as the men stared. Austin leaned over and smiled as he read the communiqué. "Bob, you might not be able to stop them, but I can."

"I don't want you doing anything stupid."

"Would you die for your kids?" he asked his friend.

"Of course."

"Would you die for your wife?"

"Yes."

"Then don't talk to me about stupid."

His buddy shook his head despairingly.

"If you don't trust my driving your car, get me a squad car," Austin said. "And an escort while you're at it."

"No, Austin, don't!"

Austin was already pushing through the milling crowd on the stairs. "In fact, a squad car is an excellent idea," he called back to Bob. "We don't have a second to spare. If Karinolov gets wind of this fax, he's just crazy enough to shoot her dead on the spot."

AT THE BOTTOM of the marble staircase, in the midst of the chaos, stood an older woman. On one arm was crooked an ornate tiger-maple cane. On her other arm, a young woman with coal-black hair and red-rimmed eyes.

Austin's eyes met those of the older woman and he realized he was staring into Tarini's eyes. Like emeralds, but with a weariness that Tarini didn't possess.

"Mrs. Schaskylavitch," he said.

She grabbed his arm with surprising strength.

"You must be Austin Smith." she said, her voice lightly accented. "You are more than a friend to my daughter. A mother knows these things."

"I am, and you're Tarini's mother?" he said,

sparing a glance at the younger woman who must be Tanya.

"Yes. Find her. Find my daughter and my... grandchild. Tanya has told me everything."

"Where did Karinolov take her?"

"He's dragging her back to Byleukrainia."

"Won't get much of a reception there," Austin observed. "Vladimir's escaped from prison and has led his supporters to the Parliament house."

The two women smiled through their tears. Austin remembered that Tarini's father had died fighting for the Romanovs so many years before. The Schaskylavitch family had been linked with the Romanovs for generations before that. Would Tarini die for the Romanovs, too?

"Do you love her?" Tarini's mother asked him.

"Yes, I do."

"Then Godspeed to you."

He felt Bob at his shoulder.

"Let's go," Austin ordered.

"Take me with you," the young girl begged, adding, "I can shoot a gun. And I know Karinolov."

Austin narrowed his eyes. Was she trustworthy? He didn't know. But at least she had the decency to blush when she mentioned Karinolov's name.

"Go," Tarini's mother urged. "I will only slow you down and you don't have much time."

Austin nodded to Bob.

"We'll take Tanya," he said, barely registering the odd look that passed between Bob and Tarini's sister.

THERE WASN'T a police officer in all of New York who could drive fast enough for Austin's tastes, so he took the wheel of squad car 435.

Bob's partner threw up his hands in frustration, but relinquished the keys out of loyalty to Austin, who had done the blues at the department so many favors. He opened the rear door for Tanya.

"This is definitely against department policy," Bob said as he threw the keys to Austin. "Civilians are never, ever, ever supposed to drive."

Austin shrugged, jumping into the driver's seat. "Make me your deputy," he said.

"Fine. You swear to uphold the law?"

"Yeah."

"All right, you're a deputy."

Austin squealed away from the curb as Bob struggled to slam his passenger-side door shut.

As they wove through traffic on Franklin D. Roosevelt Drive, Bob clung to his dashboard.

An escort of four squad cars struggled to keep up as Austin flew across midtown, taking a shortcut east and toward Kennedy Airport. He kept the siren and overhead cherries going, and after a while, didn't even notice the lights, the ear-splintering sound, the cars and pedestrians diving this way and that to stay out of his way.

Bob stayed on the radio, tracking down airport security, confirming what they already suspected: the Byleukrainian U.N. Mission was packing up and heading home. A gorgeous brunette wasn't among the mission personnel gathering to leave.

She must be in the crate, Austin thought with a tight shudder. That's if she wasn't already dead.

"They're loading at the international terminal," Bob said. "And it looks like they're trying to take the entire mission with them—all the personnel, every stick of furniture, even those beautiful paintings. But they haven't filed a flight plan."

Austin grimaced. "They must have figured on heading for Byleukrainia, but if they find out that events at the capital have turned against them, Karinolov wants his options open."

"Argentina?"

"Someplace similarly receptive to ex-soldiers with money. Someplace he can disappear. If that plane gets off the ground, it doesn't matter who's in charge of Byleukrainia, we'll never see him again. Or Tarini."

"It's all my fault," Tanya moaned from the back seat.

"You're right, it is," Austin agreed.

"Buddy, I know you're worried about Tarini—"

"And if he's not going to Byleukrainia," Austin

cut his friend off, "Tarini will just be in the way. Then we know what'll happen to her."

Bob looked at Austin. "You really do love her, don't you?"

Austin pretended he hadn't heard the question. It broke his heart to think of what might have slipped through his fingers. Because of his pride. His damnable male pride.

He leaned on the horn until a moving van blocking his way was forced off the road.

They flew up onto the median strip, sideswiping dogwood trees, and then flopping onto the blacktop, hubcap tottering off.

Austin jerked to a halt in the middle lane of the parking area outside the Central Terminal Building, leaping out of the car and vaulting over awestruck porters, with Bob huffing to keep up.

He flashed his expired Byleukrainian U.N. Mission security badge at the Marine Air Terminal security gate. A gate attendant waved him through.

"Sir, sir, you can't go in there, sir," a perky ticket attendant called as Austin shoved through a crowd gathered at the counter and threw open the steel doors behind the Byleukrainan Airlines counter.

Cold, brisk air smacked his face. He was inside an open loading hangar. A 727 with the Byleukrainian Aeroflot logo was refueling with its nose out tight on the yellow painted path to the runway. At its open luggage compartment, a conveyer belt loaded crate after crate emblazoned with colorful diplomatic-courier seals. Workers in neon orange jumpsuits carried suitcases and trunks into the front seating area.

Austin felt, rather than heard, Bob come up behind him. Tanya slid to his side.

"Bob, get the other officers in here and round these guys up," Austin said and strode toward the plane. The workers scattered and he climbed into the plane.

Outfitted for Karinolov's needs, the seats had been stripped from the coach compartment. Instead, the tunnel-like section of the plane was filled with boxes, crates, stacks of expensive oil paintings and rolled-up Bukkhara rugs.

Where was Tarini?

He tore open one crate and dropped its contents in disgust—priceless china. He yanked the lid off another and, muttering a frustrated oath, threw a sterling-silver epergne to the floor.

Then he caught sight of it. The box was larger than all the others and carefully concealed behind a stack of rugs. Austin toppled the rugs and scraped open the seal of the diplomatic crate.

"Tarini!" he shouted, cracking the boards that held the crate together. He opened it and found her, crouched into her restraints, her eyes wide and fearful. "Oh, my darling!"

He split the leather restraints with his fingers. She looked up at him, glassy-eyed and dazed, but otherwise all right. He marveled at the feel of her in the safety of his arms.

"I'm never letting go of you," he whispered in her ear. "I love you so much…"

She relaxed into his embrace and he kissed her, moaning at the sweetness of her lips. He could never be apart from her again, he knew. But he had a job to do before he could promise her a happy-ever-after. Reluctantly, he pulled away, leaving her mouth half-kissed.

"Tarini, we've got to stop Karinolov."

She nodded slowly, her eyes clouded, and Austin guessed she was desperately fighting whatever narcotic Karinolov must have given her. The same thing he had given Austin…?

He felt a sudden stab of anger—an anger on behalf of his child, who might be harmed by the drug.

"Austin, I must tell you…"

And then they heard the click of a gun. Austin felt the barrel against his neck.

His mind raced ahead and he reluctantly accepted the truth he had not wanted to believe. He thought of the sensor placed on his friend's car.

"Hello, Bob," he said without turning around.

Chapter Seventeen

This is going so much better than I planned, Karinolov thought, emerging from the cockpit. He looked at Austin kneeling with Bob's gun at the back of his neck.

A perfect end to Austin's story, he mused, the hotshot hero almost, but not quite, got his woman.

Even now, Austin held her hand, but he must certainly know he couldn't protect Tarini, and how that knowledge must pain him!

"Kill him," Karinolov said.

Bob shot him a miserable look. "I can't murder a friend."

"I'm touched by your ethical qualms," Karinolov replied. "But not enough to rescind my order. Shoot him. Now."

"I can't do it! You never told me it would come to this."

"I own you," Karinolov reminded him. "I purchased every I.O.U. you've left at the gambling casinos of the East Coast. You'll do as I say or it'll be your daughters who pay the price.''

With lightning speed, Austin leaped. One long, muscular leg whipped out from under his body, kicking Bob's gun into the air. Austin followed up with a block-and-punch combination that sent Bob sprawling. Karinolov had forgotten how skilled Austin was at karate.

Bob sputtered and lunged at Austin. The two men tumbled down the stairs out of the plane.

''Admirable ending to this little drama,'' Karinolov said. ''Couldn't have planned it better myself.''

He slammed shut the cabin door and grabbed Tarini's hand.

''No use leaving you in the cargo hold where you'll get into mischief,'' he said. ''We're past any danger of being stopped by Customs.''

Tarini struggled but was ineffective—the drug had sapped her strength.

Even now, as he felt her skin, he knew he wanted to possess her. He fought this emotion, reminding himself with loathing of Austin's child growing in her belly.

Tarini should have been his woman. She should be his reward for all he had endured.

Maybe there was a way to have her, he thought.

He shoved her into the cockpit. A small, waiflike

figure stood trembling at the navigator's table. His mind worked rapidly.

"Ah, my beautiful Tanya," he said, dropping Tarini on the cockpit floor like yesterday's garbage.

TARINI FELT a bitter taste in her mouth. She raised her head and tried to bring her eyes to focus. She shook her head in disbelief at what she was seeing.

In the tiny space of the cockpit, she saw her sister and Karinolov embrace. His mouth was on her sister's, his fingers splayed across her hips.

With an animal cry, Tarini lunged at the couple, catching Karinolov off balance.

"No! No!" Tanya screamed.

Tarini brought down Karinolov onto the pilot's seat. He gripped her as forcefully as she held him. Locked in a death grip, they fought for dominance.

"Bitch!" grunted Karinolov. He brought her head down and butted it against the control panel. A sharp crash sent stars to her head. She felt as if she was spinning.

Tarini realized it wasn't just her. The plane was torquing slowly and ponderously in the hangar. The force of her head against the control panel had set the plane on its axis.

Tanya screamed.

Karinolov cursed. The cockpit door flew open.

Suddenly Karinolov was off of her. Jerked to his feet by Austin, who punched him once, twice and a third time before Karinolov could even mutter a feeble plea for mercy. Austin dropped the man's unconscious body to a heap on the cockpit floor.

"Tarini, are you all right?" he asked, helping her up from the pilot's chair. He leaned forward, flicking the gear shaft, bringing the whirling plane to a halt.

Tarini rubbed the back of her head. No blood. "I'm okay," she sighed. "Just glad it's over. It is over, isn't it?" She looked down at Karinolov's still body.

"Yes, it's over," Austin answered. He pulled a folded paper from his back pocket and held it out to her. "It's all over."

She read the communiqué from the Byleukrainian capital, tears streaming down her face. "Oh, Austin, I'm so happy! Vlad's safe, he's the new leader of our country, and you…"

"I'm yours, Tarini," he said, kissing her tenderly.

Their pleasure was interrupted by a soft cry from beneath the navigator's table.

"Tanya!" Tarini exclaimed.

Her sister crawled out to Tarini's arms.

"I'm sorry!" Tanya moaned. "You thought I was kissing him for love, but I had Austin's gun. When he kissed me, I was going to shoot him and then…myself."

"Yourself?" Tarini cried in shock. "Why you?"

"Because I betrayed my country," Tanya said, burying her head in Tarini's shoulder. "I betrayed my family and my honor. I believed in him, Tarini, I believed everything he said."

Tarini slipped the gun from her sister's fingers and laid it on the carpet safely out of Tanya's reach, behind Karinolov's body.

"Tanya, many people believed in him," Austin said. "You're young and idealistic. You thought he had all the answers. But now you know better about him and about what he represents."

He took the communiqué from Tarini's hand and put it on Karinolov's chest.

"We'll let the police take care of him," he told the two women. "He doesn't have that precious diplomatic immunity of his anymore."

He helped Tarini to her feet and the two walked Tanya out of the cockpit. From the cabin windows, Austin could see the police handcuffing Karinolov's staff.

He watched Bob being led away and he grimaced. He would forgive his friend for betraying him to pay off his new gambling debts. He would forgive, but he didn't trust himself to talk to Bob today.

He looked across Tanya's head to Tarini. He had never known that he would or could love a woman so much. He had never known that there could be a relationship that would call forth his whole soul—

even more important than the relationship with his parents or even with Vlad.

She was his woman.

The mother of his child.

His equal partner.

And he would make her his wife.

FOOLS. Wretched Fools.

Rubbing his aching head, Karinolov read the communiqué from the Byleukrainian capital. Cursing, he ripped it to shreds. The world was run by fools. He was better. Stronger. Smarter. Forged of an iron will.

But it was over.

He would never have his capital, his country, Tarini.

His fingers coiled around the gun. He was not a quitter, because he was never willing to let his fate be decided by others. Karinolov was the master of his destiny. He closed his eyes and remembered how hard he had struggled. He thought of the arrest and deportation that was sure to be his fate. The return to the Byleukrainian capital in humiliation and defeat. To be consigned to death at the hands of his enemies. Or worse, to a lifetime behind bars. It would not end with this, he resolved.

"WHAT WILL HAPPEN to him?" Tarini asked Austin.

Austin glanced around the hangar. "The police

are busy rounding up his men, but they'll take him in soon enough," he said. "That was a pretty hard punch he took."

He leaned against a cargo box and, slipping his fingers through her jeans belt loops, pulled her to him. He ran his finger across her belly to remind himself of all that had been saved.

Tarini glanced across the hangar to where her sister huddled, crying. Tanya had asked to be alone with her thoughts.

Tarini's heart went out to her sister, but she knew Tanya was young. Time would soften her grief and self-reproach. She would survive.

She looked up into the eyes of her lover. "Did you mean what you said in the plane?"

"That I love you? Yes, I meant it. I've never said I love you to a woman before."

"If you had told me sooner, I wouldn't have lied to you."

"I didn't know any sooner," Austin confessed. "I didn't know how much you meant to me until I nearly lost you. But it won't happen again. Tarini, will you marry me?"

"Oh, yes, I will," she said, pressing her lips to his.

Austin would have deepened the kiss but Tarini pulled away. She was not so modern that kissing in front of a roomful of strangers didn't bother her.

Even if the strangers were busy cuffing Karinolov's men.

Besides, there was her sister. Cowering in a lonely corner of the hangar. Her shoulders shaking, her head bent, her weeping audible even from this distance.

"Go to her," Austin suggested. "It's all right. We have the rest of our lives to be together. She's young and thinks it's all over for her. Tell her different. Then we'd better call your mother."

"Oh, God! She must be so worried!"

"She's even more worried because her eldest daughter is going out with an American," Austin teased.

"She knows?"

"Yeah, and I think she likes me," Austin said with the brash confidence that had once annoyed her but now made her smile.

She pulled away from his embrace reluctantly. She started to walk toward her sister. But a chilling voice stopped her in her tracks.

"Tarini!"

Austin saw Karinolov at the cabin door. He saw his own gun in Karinolov's hand and recognized the look of despair and menace in Karinolov's eyes.

He reached instinctively to his shoulder holster and found it empty.

As if all time had stopped, he made his decision

rationally and without hesitation. There was no time to call on backup, no chance that the frozen-in-her-tracks Tarini would react in time.

He sprang to his feet and lunged for her, praying that he would shield or, better still, push her out of the line of fire altogether. There were only three people he would lay down his life for—his mother, his father and his friend Vladimir. And now there were four. Make that five.

The gunfire exploded just as he felt her softness crushed beneath his weight. He remembered the promise he had made her on the sidewalk just a scant day and a half before.

He would protect her and the child she carried.

He closed his eyes against the pain and the darkness he knew would soon come—and smiled the weary smile of the protector.

He had kept every promise he had made to her.

Epilogue

After the ceremony at the Saint Joseph's Basilica in Brooklyn, a reception was held at the United Nations Mission for the Sovereignty of Byleukrainia. Family, close friends and assorted dignitaries were transported by a caravan of black limousines with the Byleukrainian flag flapping on every hood.

As required by protocol, Prime Minister Vladimir Romanov stood at the head of the receiving line with the president of the United States and the first lady. Vlad wore a black serge tuxedo, sported close-cropped hair and a newly confident attitude very much befitting a prime minister.

He had accomplished so many things in the past few months—taken control of the country, presided over elections, which he handily won, and instituted the reforms that brought food to the starving and hope to the downtrodden.

But there had been unpleasant tasks, as well, in-

cluding the hush-hush transport of Andrei Karinolov's body to the rural outpost that had been his
birthplace. Anonymously, Vlad had paid for the private funeral and Karinolov's parents were given a
small stipend to ease their hardship.

It had not been the hero's death Karinolov's supporters would have expected. The suicide was difficult to accept and Vlad had resigned himself that
rumors would always contradict the truth of what
happened in the Kennedy hangar that night.

United Nations Ambassador Austin Smith stood
at his friend's side, one arm around his new bride,
the other still in a sling.

Austin marveled at how the winter months in a
wretched Byleukrainian prison had sharpened and
strengthened his friend. He watched as Vlad shook
hands and spoke a few personal words to each
guest. He realized that Vlad didn't need him quite
so much as when they had been young.

Maybe it had been for the best that Vlad had
gained control of his homeland without Austin
fighting his battles for him. After all, a man who
rules a country can't do it if he has to ask for his
friend's help every time there's a problem.

Still, the bond between the two men remained
strong. Not a day went by that they didn't confer.
About the trade issues for the tiny country, about
the political situation, about the country's position

in the community of nations, about the coming baby.

Austin looked to his left and placed a discreet kiss on the cheek of his bride. She wore the Romanov ring on her right hand, to remind her of the country for which she was the United Nations ambassador's wife. And she wore Austin's ring on her left hand, to remind her of their wedding promises.

Her face glowed and her belly strained only a little against her white organza-and-lace Cerutti gown. Because of the designer's expert stitching and the attention drawn to the gown's back by its hundred and twenty-eight buttons, Tarini's pregnancy was still a secret. But Austin was sure that soon everyone would know. And would share their joy.

The couple wouldn't have much time together, alone, before the baby came.

At Tarini's side stood her mother and sister. Austin's parents were stationed at the end of the receiving line. The former ambassador clasped hands with old colleagues and longtime friends. His father and mother had taken him aside to tell him that since Austin was now a representative of the Byleukrainian government, he was entitled to know that his mother was an occasional spy for the United States government and had been for thirty years.

"But, Dad, I've always thought it was you who…"

"Ha!" His father had laughed. "Your mother is much better at espionage than I'd ever be. Quiet and so good at drawing people out. People tell her all sorts of things, thinking she's just a bland, somewhat ditzy diplomatic wife. But she's been responsible for a number of intelligence operations."

"But your gadgets and those rumors…"

"I love to invent things," the ambassador said, "but I could never do what your mother does. Too dangerous."

Looking at his mother at the end of the receiving line, Austin reflected that she really did make a great spy. No one would suspect the demure, ever-so-proper diplomat's wife.

As the five hundred guests made their way into the ballroom, Austin noticed that Bob and his wife and daughters—Austin's goddaughters—had slipped in without going through the receiving line. Bob was avoiding him, Austin reflected, knowing that his friend still felt awful about how he had succumbed to Karinolov's blackmail. Austin reminded himself that he'd have to take Bob aside and remind him, yet again, that when he forgave a friend, he forgave…and forgot.

For now, Austin turned his thoughts to his bride.

"Tarini, let's slip out," Austin whispered. "We could go upstairs right now and…"

"But, Ambassador," she said archly, "you have all these guests to consider. The Egyptian ambassador just arrived. There'll be a diplomatic incident if you leave him without someone to talk to. Besides, the orchestra is beginning the first dance."

And protocol required that the first dance with the bride belonged to the man who gave her away. Vlad stepped out of the receiving line and shyly approached Tarini.

"May I?" he asked.

With a quick kiss to her new husband, Tarini took Vlad's arm and entered the mission's grand ballroom. After playing a few bars of the Byleukrainian national anthem to get the attention of the guests, the orchestra segued into a Chopin waltz.

Vlad, who had always been good at the skills required of a man of his station, expertly swirled Tarini around the ballroom as the guests stepped back to give them room. Tarini waved to her friends Toria and Nicholas Sankovitch, who had flown in from Chicago for the occasion though Toria was scant weeks from her due date.

"I am so happy for you and Austin," Vlad said. "It has all ended as it should have."

"Except there is one mystery left," Tarini said.

"What is that?"

"Who the dashing prime minister will ask to dance after he has danced with me," Tarini explained playfully. "I watched the morning news and the reporter was certain that it was either to be Brooke Shields—'' Tarini gestured to the staircase where the beautiful actress stood ''—or perhaps the daughter of the president.''

Vlad glanced to where the president's family stood together, but said nothing.

''The news reports also suggested you might dance with the former wife of the Prince of...''

Vlad looked over her shoulder at the divorced princess.

''Beautiful, but I've met her before,'' he said. ''Not my type.''

''So who will it be?''

''Who do you think it should be?''

''I was thinking you could ask my sister.''

''Tanya?'' Vlad laughed. ''Tanya's just a baby. She can't be more than...how old is she anyhow?''

''Twenty.''

''But she's...'' He raised his hand to his waist to indicate height, raising it another foot as Tarini shook her head. At last, he put his hand up to his shoulder with a questioning glance.

Tarini nodded. ''She's right over there,'' Tarini said, nodding toward her mother and sister. Her sister wore a pale pink dress with a tulle skirt. Tiny rosettes dotted her bodice and her long black hair.

''That's Tanya?'' Vlad exclaimed. ''When I saw her at the ceremony, I thought she was just another ravishing Schaskylavitch cousin. I couldn't imagine..."

"Imagine," Tarini said as the music died down.

"My dance," Austin insisted at their shoulder.

"Sure," Vlad said, clearly dazed, relinquishing Tarini. "Who did the news reports say I was going to dance with?"

"Brooke Shields, the president's daughter or the princess."

"Well, they're all wrong," Vlad said, sweeping across the room.

As Vlad asked Tanya to dance, an audible murmur swept through the crowd. The reporter from "Entertainment Tonight" dashed out of the room. The divorced princess quickly took the arm of the French ambassador.

"They look good together, don't you think?" Tarini said, noting the flush of pleasure on her sister's face.

"Matchmaker," Austin accused playfully.

"I just want everyone I love to be happy," Tarini said.

"We're all happy. Everything has turned out wonderfully."

"Except..."

"Except," Austin admitted, thinking of that terrible moment when he had thought he was going to die.

Karinolov had seen the future he was consigned

to, had known exactly what would await him in his homeland. The humiliation had been too much to bear—and Karinolov was not a man who could weather humiliation.

Not before a final hideous farewell to the woman he had loved. As Austin had lunged to save Tarini from what he thought was certain death, Karinolov shoved his gun into his own mouth and fired. Austin's quick reflex had been proven wrong, but he had acted from the heart—and when he had opened his eyes and known that he was not to die at Karinolov's hands, he had known that he was Tarini's.

Completely and utterly and forever.

The dance was over too quickly and Austin and Tarini parted. He danced with the women he was required to—the sulking princess, the first lady, and assorted ambassadors' wives. In deference to her wounded leg, he sat out one dance with Tarini's mother, who chatted endlessly about preparations for the baby. Austin realized it was good for her to have something nice to think about, after the long years of struggle.

He looked out on the ballroom, watching for Tarini, who had been doing her part dancing with the representatives of every country, as well as the husband of the British ambassador. He caught sight of Vlad and smiled slyly.

Vlad was dancing a second time with Tanya. Definite protocol violation.

As Tanya's brother-in-law, he'd have to have a talk with Vlad. He stood up and accepted a glass of champagne from the tray of a passing waiter.

Then he felt it.

On his wrist.

Steel clamping down with a sharp click.

"Why, Mrs. Ambassador!" he exclaimed with just the right touch of shock and outrage.

Tarini smiled mysteriously.

"Don't these come in handy?" she asked. "In the right situations, of course."

With Austin sputtering that they couldn't just leave their guests, she led him up the marble rotunda staircase to the bedroom of the private apartment on the top floor of the mission.

He looked at the sheets, rumpled from their hasty lovemaking this morning, before the ceremony. He smiled slyly as she unlocked the cuffs.

"Did I tell you today that I love you?"

"You've said it twelve times since midnight."

"Maybe I should say it one more time."

"I'd prefer to hear the words when you're more...horizontal," Tarini said playfully.

He laughed broadly and flung himself down on the bed beside her. He wondered how he would manage all hundred and twenty-eight buttons of the Cerutti creation. Then he remembered marriage is forever and Tarini wouldn't be needing this dress again.

Four months later, the United Nations Mission for the Sovereignty of Byleukrainia announced the birth of Vladimir Schaskylavitch Smith. His namesake and godfather, Prime Minister Vladimir Romanov, immediately presented young Vladimir with his own castle and a crown that had graced generations of princes in the time before democratic rule.

HARLEQUIN®

I N T R I G U E®

Cheyenne Nights

by Carla Cassidy

As little girls the Connor sisters dreamed of gallant
princes on white horses. As women they were swept away
by mysterious cowboys on black stallions. But with dusty
dungarees and low-hung Stetsons, their cowboys are no
less the knights in shining armor.

Join Carla Cassidy for the Connor sisters'
wild West Wyoming tales of intrigue:

SUNSET PROMISES
(March)

MIDNIGHT WISHES
(April)

SUNRISE VOWS
(May)

You are cordially invited to a

HOMETOWN REUNION

September 1996—August 1997

Bad boys, cowboys, babies. Feuding families,
arson, mistaken identity, a mom on the run...
Where can you find romance and adventure?
Tyler, Wisconsin, that's where!

So join us in this not-so-sleepy little town and
experience the love, the laughter and the
tears of those who call it home.

WELCOME TO A
HOMETOWN REUNION

Gossip about the fire is on the back burner
once Kika Mancini, talent scout, rolls into Tyler;
everyone's hoping to be a star. But Kika is
looking for one particular baby—Nick Miller's—
who's perfect for her client. Finding Nick is a
bonus, because he's perfect for *her,* even if he
is about to cost her her job. Don't miss
Pamela Bauer's *Fancy's Baby,* the eighth
in a series you won't want to end....

Available in April 1997
at your favorite retail store.

LOVE *or* MONEY?
Why not Love *and* Money!
After all, millionaires
need love, too!

How to Marry a MILLIONAIRE

**Suzanne Forster,
Muriel Jensen
and
Judith Arnold**
bring you three original stories
about finding that one-in-a million man!

Harlequin also brings you
a million-dollar sweepstakes—enter
for your chance to win a fortune!

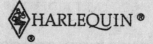

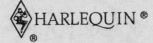

It's hot...and it's out of control!

BLAZE

Beginning this spring, Temptation turns up the *heat*. Look for these bold, provocative, *ultra*sexy books!

#629 OUTRAGEOUS
by Lori Foster (April 1997)

#639 RESTLESS NIGHTS
by Tiffany White (June 1997)

#649 NIGHT RHYTHMS
by Elda Minger (Sept. 1997)

BLAZE: Red-hot reads—only from

HARLEQUIN®
Temptation

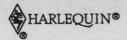